The Adventure of the Spectred Bat

Note to Readers:

Your enjoyment of this new Sherlock Holmes mystery will be enhanced by re-reading the original story that inspired this one –
The Adventure of the Speckled Band.
It has been appended and may be found in the back portion of this book.

The Adventure of the Spectred Bat

A New Sherlock Holmes Mystery

Craig Stephen Copland

Hey readers: The first day of every month is *New Sherlock Day*. All New Sherlock Holmes Mysteries ebooks on Kindle will go on sale for 99 cents for one day only. Watch for it at the start of each month.

Published by:

Conservative Growth
1101 30th Street NW. Ste. 500
Washington, DC 20007

Cover design by Rita Toews.

ISBN: 1512296821

ISBN: 978-1512296822

Dedication

Throughout the world there are countless unsung heroes, mostly women, who labor unrewarded, helping mothers safely deliver healthy happy children. This story, involving as it does, the wonders of pregnancy and childbirth, is dedicated to them.

It is absolutely not dedicated to Bram Stoker or anyone that is involved in the marketing of vampires.

Contents

Acknowledgments

As a dedicated Sherlockian I must first and foremost give credit to Dr. John H. Watson and thank him for recording the stories of the many adventures of Sherlock Holmes, and to his literary agent, Arthur Conan Doyle, for arranging to have them published in *The Strand* and in various other periodicals in America and abroad.

I must also thank the Sherlock Holmes Society of Canada, better known as The Bootmakers, for hosting a contest for the writing of a new Sherlock Holmes mystery. My successful entry into that competition led to the writing of other pastiche stories about Sherlock Holmes.

I discovered *The Adventures of Sherlock Holmes* while a student at Scarlett Heights Collegiate Institute in Toronto. My English teachers – Bill Stratton, Norm Oliver, and Margaret Tough – inspired me to read and write. I shall be forever grateful to them.

My dearest and best friend, Mary Engelking, read all drafts, helped with whatever historical and geographical accuracy was required, and offered insightful recommendations for changes to the narrative structure, characters, and dialogue. Thank you.

Many words and whole phrases and sentences have been lifted and copied shamelessly and joyfully from the sacred canon of Sherlockian literature. Should any word or turn of phrase strike the reader as the *mot juste,* you may count on its having been plagiarized.

Chapter One
How Beautiful and Terrified She Was

It has been nearly a decade, but I remember it as if it were yesterday — the day I met Sherlock Holmes. It was in a hospital laboratory and he was exulting over some new test he had found for the presence of hemoglobin. After a short and strange conversation about tobacco, bull pups, Afghanistan, and violin music we agreed to share diggings on Baker Street. Oh how little I suspected back then that my life was about to change; how it would turn topsy-turvy as I followed Sherlock Holmes all over London and beyond as he put "the science of deduction" to work in solving crimes and bringing blackguards to justice. Along the way, I was able to establish a moderately successful medical practice and a wonderfully successful reputation as a writer of mystery stories.

During those years, I have observed Holmes as he worked on behalf of over one hundred clients, none commonplace, and I have made notes on over seventy of those that were the most fascinating. I described some of these in the pages of *The Strand* and have been blessed to have found so many readers who enjoy reading about the adventures of this most unusual of men.

Yet there was one case that I have always put off telling others about. My hesitancy in doing so has not been for fear of a lack of interest from my readers. Not at all! The case was perhaps the strangest of all that I have observed and chronicled to date. No, my reasons were otherwise. In the first place, the case involved some aspects of the supernatural, or at least a belief in that realm by the client, a young woman who was about to become a mother. Given that Sherlock Holmes is such a stickler for the use of science and deduction alone in the solving of crimes, it seemed inappropriate to give even the faintest hint that anything other than rigorous human reason was ever used in any of his cases. I would not want to sully the reputation of my esteemed friend by ever suggesting otherwise.

My second reason for not having released the details of this case to the public is much more mundane. The facts, I feared, might upset the delicate constitutions of some of my readers. Your first thought is most likely that I am referring to the sensibilities of some of my female readers, whose tender hearts might be disturbed by references to cruelty and violence. But that is not it at all, I assure you. In truth, the opposite is the case. It is the men amongst my readers that I have been concerned for, especially those who are younger in years. For the story cannot be told without reference to the functions of the female body during the periods of expectancy and childbirth. To women, of course, these functions are natural. They chat amongst themselves without end about these matters in much the same way as men chat about the latest football game. Young men, however, on listening to such conversations are most likely to pale and become weak in the knees and seek immediately to excuse themselves from the room. That is the reason why every doctor or midwife I know refuses to allow fathers to be present at the birth of their children and depends solely on nurses or other mothers to assist in the delivery. It is a commonplace amongst those in the medical profession that in the delivery of children we already have two patients to care for, and do not want a third, especially if he has passed out and is lying on the floor.

Yet, if I may borrow a phrase from Mr. Carroll's Walrus, the time has come to talk of many things and place them upon a record, including the details relating to the very strange story of the Spectred Bat, so that the rumors that have grown up concerning this case might be put to flight and the truth become known. Callow lads amongst my male readers are duly cautioned that the content might be disturbing to their still sensitive young minds.

It was in the fall of 1887; more precisely in the dark small hours of the morning of Sunday, September 4 that my peaceful sojourn in the realm of Morpheus was roughly disturbed by the hand of Sherlock Holmes shaking my shoulder. In the light of the full moon streaming through my bedroom window, I could see that the clock on my wall was reading two o'clock.

"Good heavens," I cried in my semi-conscious state. "What is it? Is the house on fire?"

"Sorry to do this to you, my dear doctor," Holmes said. "But a client has arrived and I fear she may need medical attention. She is under great duress and has walked through the metropolis to Baker Street all the way from Waterloo Station."

"At this hour of the night? All by herself?" I asked in alarm.

"Indeed and she is trembling both with cold and fear. Something is terribly amiss in her life. I need your help to settle her before she is able to explain her case. Could you, my good man, rise and assist her?"

"Of course my dear fellow," I said and I rose and quickly pulled on my clothes and made my way to the front room of 221B Baker Street. There, sitting on the settee in front of the hearth and dressed in black was a young woman, perhaps twenty years of age at the very most. The ever-attentive Mrs. Hudson was already ministering to her and had wrapped the poor thing in a blanket and brought her some hot tea and honey and lit the fireplace. Her body was shivering and shaking uncontrollably, causing her long waves of raven hair to jump and bounce as if attached to an elastic cord. Most remarkably, she was quite obviously expecting a child. Even with her wearing loose-fitting clothes I could see that she was no more than a few weeks away from giving birth. She looked at me as I sat down beside her and her dark blue eyes, which at other times would have been irresistibly beautiful, conveyed a presence of profound terror in her soul.

"Miss," said Holmes. "This is my colleague, Dr. Watson. You may have complete confidence, as I do, in his discretion as well as in his medical abilities. Please. There is no rush. You are safe here. We can wait until you are able to compose yourself."

"Th...th...thank you," the girl stuttered as she continued to shiver and shake. I took her pulse and held her cold hand in mine and concluded that she was of sound body and not facing any immediate medical emergency. So for the next five minutes, Holmes and I just sat in silence while Mrs. Hudson vigorously rubbed the girl's back and kept her cup filled. Eventually, her pitiable state of agitation and shivering subsided and she looked up at Sherlock Holmes.

"I am so sorry... Please forgive me! I am so sorry, but I was terrified and had nowhere else to turn. I am so sorry to have disturbed you in the middle of the night. I'm so sorry."

"It is quite alright, Miss," said Holmes warmly. "It is our responsibility and privilege to assist a young woman in desperate need, as I perceive you are. Please, just try to settle yourself, and tell me what has brought you all the way from Surrey at this hour of the night."

I have watched on many occasions as Sherlock Holmes revealed that he already knew more about a client that he had been told, all by means of his exceptional powers of observation and deduction. Most clients merely looked surprised when he subjected them to his unusual ability, but this young woman reacted in sheer terror.

"Dear God," she gasped in a low voice. "You're one of them. You're one of them. You were my only hope and you are one of them."

"My dear young lady," I said as I took her trembling hand in both of mine. "One of whom? This man is Mr. Sherlock Holmes, the well-known detective, and I am Dr. Watson. We are none other than who we are."

"You are one of them. You are one of them, who know things that it is impossible to know except that the evil spirit world has revealed them to you. Dear God, help me." Her shivering from the cold had subsided, but now her body was trembling in fear. Her hands were on the arms of the chair, ready to lift her up and out of the room. Fortunately, Mrs. Hudson stepped in, leaned down towards the frightened young girl and placed both of her warm hands on the cheeks of the beautiful but drawn and gray face.

"No. No, my dear. He is not anything like that. He is just a bit of a strange man who likes to show off his smartness and there is nothing at all about him that is anything but human. So please, just be at peace and he will tell you how he knew about you, and then he will do whatever he can to look after you." She gave a sharp look to Holmes, which commanded him not to do anything else that might upset the fearful soul.

"I assure you," said Holmes, somewhat chagrined, "I have no supernatural abilities whatsoever. I merely observed that you arrived at our door at precisely 1:45 in the early morning and that your overcoat and stockings had acquired numerous small pieces of vegetation. These could not have become attached to you had you walked to Baker Street through any of the streets of London other than those that border on Hyde Park. There is a portion of a train ticket protruding from your purse and therefore, you must have come here directly from a station. The only station that is in the direction past Hyde Park is Waterloo, and it serves trains coming from the Southwest. You boarded the last train of the night in Leatherhead or Sutton and made your way on foot to Baker Street as there would be no cabs working at this hour. My knowing this is nothing more than a process of observation and logic. I regret having disturbed you. Please, explain your situation to us and we will do whatever is possible to help and protect you and your child."

She continued to look fearful and ready to bolt from the room. Once again Mrs. Hudson intervened and stood behind her, placing her friendly hands on the girls' shoulders and speaking quietly into her ear. "Dearie, it is quite alright. These men will look after you, as will I. Now just close your eyes, take a very deep slow breath, and then let us hear your story."

The young woman lifted one of her hands to her shoulder and placed it on top of Mrs. Hudson's. She kept it there as she looked at Holmes and began to speak.

"I know of you, sir, from the stories in *The Strand,* and from a personal recommendation from a neighbor of mine, Mrs. Farintosh. You helped her after the untimely death of her husband when his business partners attempted to defraud her of her shares in the local milling company. She said that you were exceedingly odd but to be trusted and so I have come to you, and I confess that I am in fear and have come in panic. I have nowhere else to turn. The police will dismiss me as having a temporary madness brought on by my pregnancy."

"That," said Holmes, "is only one of the silly notions held by men who are police officers, and they are not alone. I do not share their convictions. Pray, proceed."

She closed her eyes again for several seconds, took another deep breath, and then looked at Holmes directly and said, "A month ago my sister was killed by a vampire and now it is trying to kill me."

I confess that my first reaction was to say to myself, "Oh dear. We have a fruit-cake on our hands at two o'clock in the morning... now what?"

Sherlock Holmes, though I know him as well as he can be known, surprised me. I was quite certain that the vampire was sufficient grounds for him to dismiss this wild-eyed young woman, but instead, he looked at her and in a matter-of-fact tone inquired,

"You say your sister was killed. Tell me the details of what happened. Please try to be as precise and exact as you can remember."

The young woman's face relaxed visibly and she closed her eyes and nodded slowly. She released her grip on the hand of Mrs. Hudson. "Thank you, sir. Yes, sir, here are the reasons for my terror and my disturbing you.

"One month ago my sister, my twin sister Julia that is, died in my arms. She was also expecting a child, although she was further along in her condition than I was. That fatal night, the night of the fourth of August, my sister could not sleep well. There was a strange odor in the house, as if one of the fireplaces had been blocked and rubber was burning and the smoke not escaping. She knocked on the door of my bedroom at close to eleven o'clock and told me that she was going for a walk in the moonlight to find some fresh and cleaner air. It was a warm and brightly lit summer evening and I had no feeling of impending misfortune, but as I had already retired for the evening, I did not join her and returned to my bed.

About an hour later I heard her scream. I had heard my sister shout or scream or cry in the past, as all sisters do when growing up so closely together, and as twins, we shared those subtle links which bind two souls, which are so closely allied. But this was unlike anything I had ever heard in my life. It was a loud scream of unspeakable terror. I rose from my bed just as I heard her pounding on my door and shouting my name. As I opened the door, she threw herself into my arms. Her eyes were wide with fear like those of a hunted animal and she was shaking throughout her body. "What is it?" I cried to her. 'Julia, what is it?'

"Oh my God, Helen! It attacked me. It bit me.' 'What did? Sister, tell me,' I begged her. 'The vampire. The vampire bat. It bit me while I was walking in the laneway. The gypsies sent it. A vampire has taken my life. Sister, do not let me die. Do not let my baby die."

"She was sore and distressed and my first thought was to comfort her and so I told her that it was only a specter, an illusion brought on by the imbalance of hormones that accompanies pregnancy. I just held her close and tried to soothe her, but she

7

screamed back at me. 'No! No!' she shouted. 'Look. It attacked me. It bit me. It has taken my life.'

"She put her fingers to her neck and I could see two small wounds, close to one another, as if she had been wounded by a set of pins. There was a small trickle of blood dripping from them. 'And look. Here,' she said and she opened her night dress and exposed her left breast. Directly on the lower portion, I could see two more small wounds, again close together and with drops of blood coming from them. Her face was blanched with terror. 'Suck the poison out,' she said to me in a desperate voice. 'Sister, suck out the poison or else I am dead. The vampire has taken me. Suck the poison, I beg you.'

"I then thought that she had been bitten by an insect or something else such as unpleasant but not dangerous, and so to help calm her spirit, I did as she requested, first on her neck and then on her breast. I sucked some of her blood and spat it out. But as I did so I could feel that her pulse was racing uncontrollably and that her breathing was becoming labored.

She writhed as one who is in terrible pain. It was then that I knew that she was truly in danger. I shouted for the help and then continued to suck and spit out her blood as hard as I could. A maid soon appeared and I sent her into the village to fetch the doctor. Then Julia lost her consciousness, her knees seemed to give away, and I held her and shouted to her. "Julia! Wake up! Keep breathing, the doctor is coming.'

For the next ten minutes I continued to minister to her. Another maid brought some smelling salts, but it was all for naught. She ceased her breathing. A few minutes later her pulse faded and vanished. By the time the doctor arrived she was gone. Such was the dreaded end of my beloved sister. I was beside myself with grief and had collapsed to the floor, holding the lifeless body of my dearest love in my arms."

At this point in her story she ceased speaking and dropped her lovely face into her hands and wept. Mrs. Hudson, who had stepped into the kitchen but had been listening to the young woman's story, came back into the front room and placed another cup of tea in front of the poor thing. I could tell from the faint wafting scent of the tea that she had fortified it not only with honey but with a wee bit of brandy as well. The terrified young woman took a slow sip and then again began to speak.

"The doctor pronounced her dead. He examined her and said that she had only been bitten by some sort of flying insect and that the fright, coming as it did during a period of excited hormones, had brought about heart failure. We buried her the next day, with her child still in her womb. The priest conducted the funeral and the burial according to the missal but said no words nor made any of the rituals that are required when warding off vampires. I hope and pray that the soul of my dear sister has gone into eternity and I feel a terrible dread that she has been taken by the vampire world and will remain among the un-dead for centuries to come."

Here Holmes spoke up, again with nothing but reassuring acceptance in his voice. "I know that this has been very difficult for you. But please continue. Why did you arrive here at this hour? What brought about your flight into London all alone, so far along in your period of expectation, and unaccompanied?"

Again, her face took on a look of fear and the blood drained from her countenance. "Earlier this evening it attacked me. The vampire bat attacked me as I was walking home from the village. I had been there to visit a friend, the wife of my former employer, and was walking back to the house. Evening had just fallen, but it was still light enough to walk. As I entered our laneway, I chanced to look up and saw a bat flying directly toward me. I threw myself to the ground as it passed and then I rushed into the fencerow beside the lane and hid amongst the trees and bushes. I moved along on my hands and knees so that I could not be seen. I know that ordinary bats are blind and can attack without seeing, but I know that a vampire bat has the sense of sight. It took me over an hour to make my way back out through the copse of trees and onto the road and then I ran all the way back into the village."

"And why," asked Holmes, "did you not return to your house?"

"On Saturday evenings, the help are given time off and return to their homes in the village. My stepfather was away, as he often is on weekends. I knew that there was no one there to assist me and so I ran, as quickly as someone in my condition is able to, directly to the train station and waited in the passengers' room until the late train appeared. I boarded it and came straightaway to London and then hurried my way through the night to your address.

"Had I stayed in Surrey I knew that the vampire would find me, and I would die, along with my child, just as my sister had. I had your address as I said from Mrs. Farintosh, and I came here directly, stopping only along the way once or twice to ask directions from some of the ladies who were on the streets."

Holmes looked upon her with one of his quick and all comprehensive glances. "It is well you came here. I do believe that your life may be in danger and I assure you that we will provide the protection you seek. Now my dear, having bravely gotten through the most difficult parts of your story we can now move to the less troublesome. You said your sister blamed the gypsies. What gypsies?"

"There has been a band of them on the estate property for as long as I can remember. My stepfather has a fondness for them and allows them to stay."

"Ah yes. Now then, about your stepfather, your life in Surrey, and your child that will soon be arriving. Please, as concisely as you can, inform us of your history and the events that pertain to your case."

"Yes sir, I will do as you say. I believe I can still my heart and start my story at the beginning and try to be straightforward."

"I am all attention," said Holmes.

Chapter Two
Loved by the Guards

The fearful young raven-haired beauty continued her story. "My name is Helen Stoner. I have, or I should say I had, until a month ago, a twin sister, Julia. My father was from an old established family and he served in the Foreign Office. Our family lived in several countries according to his posting.

When my sister and I were just seven years of age he was sent to Bucharest, in Romania. Our life there was pleasant and I can remember our wonderful vacations near Constanza on the Black Sea and I remember the Gypsy musicians and dancers. When we had both just turned nine years of age he just suddenly died. I do not know the details of his death as our mother never disclosed them to us. She was very preoccupied, what with two young daughters and all the stressful things that had to be done. While living there, however, our family had made use of the services of a local doctor named Dr. Romanescu. He came to our aid and looked after all the necessary arrangements for the shipping of my father's body back to England and our safe return to our homeland. He even accompanied us first to London and then to Surrey where we set up our home in the pleasant estate of Stoke Moran that had been in my father's family for many years. My mother was exceedingly grateful to Dr. Romanescu and must have become quite fond of him, as she married him just six months later."

"Please," interrupted Holmes, "pardon my intrusion into your account, but do I understand you to be telling me that you have no knowledge concerning your father's sudden death?"

"My sister and I were only children at the time and my mother must have wished to spare us the pain that such details would have brought to our young hearts. All I remember is that my father was a fit and vigorous man who played with us joyfully when he was not traveling. But one day, while he was away in some other part of the country, my mother informed us that instead of returning to see us in Bucharest, my Father had gone to live with Jesus in heaven and would not be coming back, but that we would see him again when we went to heaven. That was all we were told."

"Surely, though, since reaching adulthood she has told you more than that. Surely you and your sister asked her what happened to your father."

"No sir. Not because we were not curious and wanted to know, but because my mother also died two years later, by which time she had still told us nothing."

"Indeed. How sad for you and your sister. How did your mother die?"

Here the young woman paused before answering. "Sir, I do not know. We were both eleven years old at the time and grown up enough to understand sickness and death or tragic accidents. All we knew is that when we came down one morning for breakfast our stepfather, Dr. Romanescu that is, told us that our mother had suddenly died in her sleep and had gone to live with Jesus in heaven and that we would see her when we went there to join her. We were stunned and terribly grieved, but no more information was ever given to us. In the years since, when we ventured to inquire, our stepfather, who now insisted that we call him "Father", told us that we should not be worrying our young minds about it, and that he was now our father and was providing a home and a life for us, and that he was wounded when we asked about our parents, for it showed that we did not love or accept him in spite of all he had done for us. This response, or some version of it, was what we received on any occasions when we made inquiries."

"Did you and your sister not talk about this matter between yourselves?"

"Why, of course, we did... many, many times. We determined that once we were either married or became of age, we would investigate the matter, but that day has not yet arrived and so I remain in the dark."

"Very well," acknowledged Holmes. "Please continue. Explain what took place in your lives after the death of your mother and please be as accurate but as brief as you are able."

"Of course, sir. From that time on we, that is my twin sister and I, had what I now understand to have been a very unusual upbringing. We were not allowed to attend school with the other children of the village but were instructed by governesses. All of them were from the Continent and related in some way to Dr. Romanescu. One was his sister, another two were his cousins, and the fourth was the sister-in-law of yet another cousin. All were from my stepfather's home city, Cluj-Napoca in the northwest of the Kingdom of Romania. They were not overly strict, but we knew very little about them before they arrived and very little more when they left us. But they did teach us our Latin and Greek, as well as French and Romanian, and also some Hungarian They instructed us in our maths and sciences; somewhat unenthusiastically in the history and culture of England, and very enthusiastically in the same subjects as they pertained to Romania, especially to the region of Transylvania, of which they were native."

"As would be expected," said Holmes, "from governesses from that part of Europe. Now, what about your father? Explain his role in your lives."

"Our stepfather ... we, my twin sister and I that is, never called him our father except when speaking to him. We had, at his insistence, very little intercourse with other children or their families, except some of the Gypsies, and so we had no basis on which to judge him. The local people that we did meet, the gardeners and the merchants, all led us to believe that he was a most unusual man. He claimed to be a medical doctor and had a certificate mounted in his study from a college in Oradea, but we never saw a single patient come to our house, nor did he ever leave the estate announcing that he was going to visit someone who was shut-in or assist in the birth of a baby, as we came to understand that other doctors spend their time doing."

She looked in my direction when she made this statement and I gave a nod of affirmation.

"Most of his days were spent in the managing of the estate property and the affairs of the firm and assets that had belonged to our father. Other than the Gypsies that camped on the edge of the estate, our stepfather had few friends and his only sport or passion was fishing. On almost every weekend other than in the wintertime, he would be gone to some part of the country to fish. Several times a year he would leave Surrey and travel, he said, to Scotland, or the east of France, or back to Transylvania. He must be quite good at it since he has several trophies and many books about the sport, and is forever, when he is at home and not working on the affairs of the firm, tying flies and practicing casting them out by the pond. He seems quite obsessed with his sport and neither my sister nor I ever objected to his so being, as the time he spent away or back at the pond was time he was not in the house. The help and the governesses were much more relaxed when he was not present and those times were far less stressful to all of us."

"Stressful, you say," queried Holmes. "Is this man a tyrant? Did he shout and threaten you or the staff? Were you beaten?"

Miss Stoner looked briefly at the floor before turning her eyes towards Holmes. "If you were to meet him, sir, you would say that he is the meekest and most humble of men. He never raises his voice and neither I nor my sister ever saw him lift a hand against us or any of the help. And yet, sir … and yet … he controlled every aspect of our lives and of the family firm, and the estate. Should my sister or I or any of the help ever do anything he did not agree with he quietly took us aside and made it very clear to us that we must not act that way again and he invoked quite severe punishments. Not of the physical kind but the revoking of any of the few privileges we enjoyed, or assigning arduous and unpleasant duties, and he watched over us until he was satisfied that every jot and tittle of the punishment had been fulfilled. In his dealings with the firm or with the local tradespeople he did likewise, never raising his voice but he made very sure that his demands, all issued quietly mind you, were met, and woe betide those who crossed him."

"In what way Miss?" asked Holmes.

At this point, I noticed a flush in Miss Stoner's young face. For several seconds, she closed her eyes and then took a quiet, deep breath before answering. "I know, sir, that if I am to receive your help, and I am desperate for it, that I must not withhold any information from you, shameful though it may be to confess it."

"You are correct in that matter," Holmes replied, "and you are assured that whatever you say will be held in complete confidence, as is the situation with every client who has ever sat in this room. Please continue."

"Beginning two years ago, when my stepfather took himself off on one of his fishing expeditions, we, my twin sister and I that is, would, late at night, enter his study and read through his business papers, his correspondence, and his financial records. It was a terrible and underhanded thing to do, but we reasoned that the estate and the shares in the firm were ours by inheritance and would come into our possession as soon as we married or reached the age of twenty-one and that we had a right to know the state our affairs were in. My stepfather would never divulge anything related to these matters to us and on the few occasions when we asked him he took offense, quietly and firmly as is his manner, but he made us feel quite wretched for having not trusted him and stepped beyond the bounds of our roles as dutiful daughters."

"His manners," said Holmes, "we can talk about later. For now, simply explain what you found in the files. Were you alarmed by the state of affairs? Was the estate and your inheritance threatened with financial ruin?"

"No sir, although we were not trained in accounting or the management of finances we could see plainly that two years ago the estate was crushed under a heavy mortgage. There had been some frightening letters from creditors demanding payment of debts long past due and threatening to seize the property. In the past twenty-four months though, the income had risen quite sharply, all of the creditors were paid off, and surplus income had been invested in securities and bonds. But we also…"

"Forgive me, again, miss," said Holmes. "What was this firm of which you speak?"

"It operates under the name of *Medical Miracles of Mole Valley*. Perhaps you are aware of it, Dr. Watson. It manufactures several secret medicinal treatments and sells them to individuals and residences throughout Britain, primarily through the mail."

The blank look on Holmes's face said that he had never heard of the firm. I, on the other hand, was quite familiar with it and not pleased to hear its name. I made a note in my mind to consult with Holmes as soon as the interview with the vampire's victim had concluded.

"In his accounts, we also read of payments, not large ones, made to several of the local men and to the leader of the gypsies. It was very strange because the local men who had been paid were not the upright men of the village, nor the skilled tradesmen. They were men whom everyone feared. They were known to be violent and likely to give a decent man a beating. Indeed, there had been stories of some of the good lads having been their victims and having been beaten within an inch of their lives. We assumed that he hired ruffians to deal with his adversaries. It troubled us that our money was being given away, even though the sums were not large."

"Your father's hirelings and the protection of your money is a matter we can address in the future," said Holmes. "Please, for now, other matters are more pressing. Who is the father of your child and why is he not providing accommodation and protection for you?"

"Really, Holmes," I blurted out. "Miss Stoner is under duress. Surely such a delicate topic can wait until she has had some rest and calmed her spirits."

Holmes gave me a bit of a quizzical look and was about to say something when the young lady herself spoke up. "Thank you Doctor, but it need not worry you. I may as well tell my whole story now as drag out the embarrassment and humiliation." She smiled warmly at me and then turned her eyes back to Holmes. "As I have told you, our stepfather was not a man of violent temper yet he was exceedingly cruel in many ways. He constantly told my sister and me that we were plain and unattractive and not particularly bright and that he despaired that any men would ever want us as wives. Our governesses told us the same thing. So we grew up believing that we were indeed not pleasant to look at and that our prospects were terribly limited. From time to time, some of the people from the local village told us what pretty girls we were, but we knew or thought we knew, that they were only being polite to the step-daughters of their employer.

A year ago a new public house, The Crown, opened in the village and the owner advertised for barmaids. Our father assumed, correctly, that the only customers who might frequent the place would be some of the laborers from the nearby farms and so he sent us to apply. I am certain that he thought he could marry us off to a couple of the duller local lads and continue to keep us near to him and under his control. To our surprise, the publican, Mr. Matthias, hired us immediately and gave us the necessary training and acted as if we were a blessing to his business. For the first time in our lives, we were able to chat and laugh with other young men and women. We were terribly nervous, but we soon relaxed and began to enjoy our tasks. Then, unbeknownst to our stepfather, a unit of the Coldstream Guards was stationed nearby for some sort of special exercises, and wasn't The Crown filled with young gentlemen officers. They chatted merrily with us and said things in French or even Latin to each other that they thought we could not understand and they were surprised when we not only understood but answered them back. Well then, some of them even began to flirt and appear to be quite fond of us.

"Mr. Matthias could see what was happening and he and his wife quite encouraged it. They had taken a bit of a shine to Julia and me and were quite pleasant to us and said that this would be our only chance to improve our situations and marry up, as they say. First, my sister became quite romantically attached to a young officer, a Peter Bennion-Bowen of Stoke-on-Trent whose family has interests in shipping pottery all over the world. Shortly thereafter, I was courted, if you can call taking a barmaid out for a walk in the moonlight courting, by Percy Armitage of Crane Water, near Reading, whose family is quite wealthy from the manufacture of bicycles. Looking back, my sister and I were babes in the woods and so when these young intoxicated men declared their love to us, making remarks of how beautiful we were, we had no means with which to defend our honor and so they, as they say, had their way with us. First my sister, and then I succumbed and both of us became with child as a result. Do I make myself plain, Sir?"

"Perfectly so."

"Our stepfather knew nothing of what had happened until one of the staff told him that my sister had begun to show, and then the truth came out. He was outwardly calm, but we could sense that he was angered beyond words. He made immediate arrangements to have us sent away to one of those homes where fallen young women are kept until the time of their delivery. Our babies would be given up for adoption and our stepfather assured us that this was the only course of action available to us and best for all concerned.

"But Mr. Matthias and his wife intervened and would not stand for it. He went immediately to the commanding officer of the Guards and demanded that the two young officers live up to their responsibilities. The major in charge of their unit called both of them onto the carpet and marched them back to their respective families and demanded that as proper Englishmen and officers in the Coldstream Guards they do the honorable thing and marry us and accept their roles as fathers.

My sister's future mother-in-law was livid and objected most vociferously. She accused Julia of being nothing more than a common whore. The father, however, understood the law and the obligations and the need for preserving the honor of such a famous regiment. As Peter was not the eldest son the family fortune was not at risk, and so his father agreed to the marriage.

"Our stepfather endeavored strenuously to stop the marriage from going ahead, but the Bennion-Bowen family is wealthy and quite influential, and the honor and reputation of the Guards was at stake, so his objections were over-ruled. A quiet, private wedding was to be conducted for my sister two weeks ago., It was not how Julia, nor I for that matter, had expected our lives to be lived, but we reasoned that a young bride could very well have to live with a miserable mother-in-law who was poor, or an equally miserable one who was rich and that it was better to have a rich one. So we were both quite happy with our prospects. But now … but now she is dead and gone. A dense darkness surrounds me, and I fear that my baby and I will not live to see my wedding either. The vampire is going to kill us both."

Chapter Three
The Humble Stepfather

Having said these words she again lost her composure and began to sob, and again Mrs. Hudson emerged from the kitchen and rubbed her shoulders and spoke a few words of comfort to her. Holmes waited patiently for the period of distress to run its course and then spoke quietly to Miss Stoner.

"Miss Helen," he began. "You are quite certain that both your sister's death and the attack upon you were by a vampire in the form of a bat. Is that correct?"

She looked up. "Yes, Mr. Holmes that is what I said for that is what happened."

"Are you aware, Miss, that many people do not believe in the existence of vampires? They are quite certain that there is no such thing."

"I have become aware of that most recently, sir, since we had conversations about them with some of the patrons of the pub. But the same fools, who have said in their hearts that there is no God, have also said that the demons and vampires and other forces of evil do not exist, but I know in my heart that they do."

"Permit me to ask you, miss, if you remember when you first began to learn about vampires?"

She was silent as if reflecting on her past. "I would have to say that I first heard of them from our governesses. They told us many stories of men and women who gave themselves to the devil and then lived forever as vampires. I must assume that my mother never told us about them as we were too young back then to understand. And yes, I clearly remember our stepfather reading to us the story of Carmilla, which had been recorded by Dr. Hesselius. How the girl who was really Mircalla had never died and returned as a vampire to the ancient ruins of Karnstein, and befriended the beautiful but innocent Laura and pierced her breast and neck as if with burning needles. Surely you know that account, do you not sir?"

"Indeed, I am familiar with it."

"And of course," she continued, "you must have read the story that just became known this past year of Count Dracula? Even the people in our village had heard the story and knew the details of it by heart. That story proved that a vampire can transform itself into a bat and attack young women. And that is what happened to my sister, and to me. It was just like the attack by the vampire bat in the story of Count Dracula. You must have read it, Mr. Holmes."

"Ah yes, a most incredible story."

"And everyone knows, do they not, that Gypsies are in league with vampires. They were the servants of Count Dracula. As children, we learned from the Gypsy children about Sara, the Black Goddess of the Gypsies. She was baptized by the Virgin Mary herself and pretended to be a virginal bride, but on her wedding nights she sucked the blood and the life force from her husbands and destroyed them. Wherever there are Gypsies, sir, there are bound to be vampires nearby."

"Is that so?"

22

"Sir, I am in your hands. Can you protect me from it? Can you find some garlic and post it around the doors and windows? Please, sir. What if the bat flies from Surrey all the way to London? They can do that, can they not? Or the Gypsies come and bring the vampires with them?"

"We will do whatever is necessary to keep bats and all such nasty things away from you. Have no fear. But you must not return yet to Surrey. It is not safe for you to be there. You may rest here on the couch until morning, at which time we will find safe lodgings for you."

Upon hearing this Mrs. Hudson again intervened and said, "She will do no such thing. She will come and stay with me in my flat, sir. It is not appropriate for a young woman to be sleeping in the quarters of two bachelors. Come lassie, give me your hand. I have a spare room and it shall be yours for now."

She took Miss Stoner's hand and helped her stand up and then led her out of the door and down the stairs to her rooms. I was left staring at Holmes in bewilderment.

"Merciful heavens, Holmes. The girl is mad. Surely you cannot be planning to take on a case that involves running from Gypsies, chasing vampires, and posting bulbs of garlic around the door. She may be under a spell of fear and indeed terror, but what she has told you is complete nonsense."

"My good doctor, you are quite correct. There is no such thing as a vampire, let alone one that can transform itself into a bat and attack people. The Roma people are strange to us but do not send bats to kill their neighbors. Those parts of the story we must put aside. What cannot be denied is that her sister, a healthy young woman, suddenly died of no apparent cause. Do young patients of yours with healthy hearts suddenly have hormonal attacks and die?"

"No. That part is troubling."

"There was a small piece in one of the papers some weeks back that gave a notice of her death and made mention of suspicions of the local Gypsies. I remember thinking at the time that there seemed to be unanswered questions, and now these deep waters have arrived on our doorstep. So, my friend, it is now past three o'clock in the morning and I suggest you get some sleep so that upon waking you will be ready to investigate this spectred bat."

I turned and began to head back to my room. Holmes sat down in his chair and lit his pipe and I knew that he would not sleep again for many hours.

Holmes kindly let me rest until half-past seven o'clock before waking me up. "Up, my friend. Come, the game is afoot. Breakfast will be laid out shortly and we have work to do and data to gather. Please, my friend. Up you get."

I rose and prepared quickly for the day and enjoyed a tasty if rapidly devoured morning meal and coffee that Mrs. Hudson, who I suspected had not slept much either, had dutifully prepared. She had no sooner cleared off the table when there came a knocking to the door on Baker Street. The good lady hustled down the stairs and returned bearing the card with the name of a Dr. Romanescu, accompanied by several letters after his name and an address near Leatherhead in Surrey.

"Ah, yes," said Holmes. "My Irregulars informed me that Miss Stoner had been followed and that we have been watched since her arrival. A rough looking chap has been loitering on the corner of Park Road for several hours. One of our doctor's employees, I suspect. This should be interesting."

I leaned close to Holmes's ear and made a trumpet of my hand. "What will you say about his daughter," I whispered. "She is still just down a floor in Mrs. Hudson's flat, is she not?"

"Daughter?" said Holmes with a sly smile. "What daughter?" Then he turned to our landlady. "My dear Mrs. Hudson, please show the gentleman in."

Appearing in our doorway was a well-dressed gentleman, somewhat shorter than me and quite a bit thicker in the torso. He had a complexion that was darker than average for someone living in England, bushy eyebrows, deep-set bile-shot eyes, a low forehead and a full head of thick, wavy black hair. He was holding his nicely brushed hat in front of his chest with both hands. He bowed rather deeply first towards Holmes and then towards me. "Gentleman," he said with an accent from the eastern regions of the Continent. "Please forgive my interrupting you so early in the morning. Might one of you be Mr. Sherlock Holmes?"

"I am Holmes," said my companion. "And whom do I have the honor of addressing?"

"I am Doctor Grigore Romanescu. And you sir," he continued, looking in my direction, "must be Dr. Watson, the very famous writer who has told the world of the brilliant adventures of Mr. Sherlock Holmes."

"I am indeed, sir. And you flatter me. I am no more than a humble recounter of the mystery stories with which my companion's excellent detective work has furnished me."

"You are both quite esteemed men," he responded. "I am but a humble country doctor attending to the health of the good folk in Surrey. It is most unusual for me to seek an appointment with gentlemen such as yourselves in London and again, please forgive me for interrupting your important affairs, but a matter of great urgency has led me to come and speak to you."

"Are you," asked Holmes, all innocence, "in need of my services? If so, please be advised that there is a bit of a queue in front of you. The English, you know, always have some problem or other vexing them and demanding my investigations. Is there a crime of which you have been or may soon be the victim? Have you been robbed?"

"Oh, no sir. My life is too insignificant to become the target of any criminals. They would have nothing to gain by robbing me. I come out of immediate concern for my daughter."

"Your daughter, you say. Oh dear, has she been robbed? Has she been dealt with unfairly by an employer? What sir, has happened to your daughter? Pray, tell me."

"My daughter sir is Miss Helen Stoner. I have reason to believe that she may have come here last evening telling you a fanciful story and seeking your services."

"Miss Stoner is your daughter?" said Holmes with an air of mild astonishment. "My good doctor, she said that she was an orphan and that her father had died over a decade ago. How can you possibly be her father?"

"Of course, Mr. Holmes, Forgive me. You are correct, as I should have known such a famous detective would be. She became my daughter legally when her mother, my dear wife, passed away into eternity several years ago."

"Ah, then you are her stepfather. Why did you not say so, sir? You had me terribly confused there. So do tell, sir, what is the issue with your stepdaughter?"

He had again bowed formally toward Holmes while speaking and then continued. "As I said sir, I believe that she may have come here last evening bearing an absurdly fanciful tale of vampires and vampire bats and claiming, most outrageously that her life was in danger. As you could see, Sir, and as you no doubt know, Dr. Watson, much better than I, she is quite heavy with child and the hormonal changes that her body is experiencing invite sudden specters and hallucinations and no end of the fancies, imaginary fears, and illusions of a nervous woman. I am here to apologize to you for her disturbing you and to convince her to return to the love and safety of her home. We are all terribly worried and concerned for her."

"Vampires and vampire bats," uttered Holmes in well-feigned astonishment. "My goodness, Dr. Romanescu, wherever did you get such strange ideas? Your step-daughter had no such concerns. She presented herself as a very sensible and unimaginative type and I am somewhat hesitant to take on the matter she presented to me."

The look of bewilderment on our visitor's face was amusing, but I was careful to give away nothing by my facial expression and sat with my hands folded in my lap, nodding solemnly.

After a second's pause, the doctor recovered and continued.

26

"Forgive me, again, sir. May I be so bold as to inquire then as to why she came to you?"

"You must forgive me," said Holmes. "But the confidentiality between me and my clients is a sacred trust and simply cannot be violated. I trust that you will accept that, sir, as I am sure you maintain the same trust between your good self and your patients."

"Yes, yes, absolutely. Except of course when my patients are not yet of age and their mothers and fathers are legally responsible for their care and the consequences of their actions. As I am sure you could see that Helen was quite young you must, as would be your duty, have inquired concerning her age and know that she is still legally under my charge. You did discern that did you not, Mr. Holmes?"

"Of course, of course. You are quite then within your rights to make such inquiries, doctor. Your daughter was very distressed, fearing that the family of the young man who is the father of her child might attempt to persuade their son to abandon her and evade their responsibilities for the support of her and the child. And so she was asking for my services regarding what avenues of legal assistance were available to her. It is an all-too-common thing these days. Our youth, I am afraid, have lost all restraint when it comes to controlling their animal spirits and I have had several young women, usually accompanied by their terribly distraught mothers, seeking my services on such measures. However, as there are available remedies in law for such conflicts I always refer them over to the offices in Chancery, although I am fearful that the bills paid to lawyers these days would devour most of the support they secured from the families of the fathers."

"My daughter was seeking help with respect to patrimonial support?" asked the Romanian. "*De necrezut.* And what did you tell her? Where did she go from here? Is she still on the premises?"

"Really, doctor. My colleague and I are bachelors and it would be most unseemly for us to permit an unchaperoned young woman to remain here during the night. Our landlady took her in and first thing this morning showed her out the back door into the laneway,

27

with instructions to secure a cab over to Chancery. She said that a rather unsavory chap had followed her from the train station. As a country girl, she seemed somewhat uncomfortable here in London. I expect, sir, that she will return to Surrey by this evening. You needn't concern yourself. She is quite a sensible young woman. Now, are you in need of a cab?"

I could see a flash of anger in the eyes of our visitor. His false humility and obsequious behavior had obviously not achieved its intended result. He retained his composure, however, and bowed to Holmes and to me as he backed toward the door. "Thank you, sir. Again, I am so sorry to disturb you and I thank you for the wise advice you gave to my daughter. A father's heart is easily agitated when his daughter is upset, and I hope you will understand and forgive my actions on behalf of my daughter and my soon-to-arrive grandchild. Good day, gentlemen."

He put on his hat and turned and descended the stairs. I got up and watched from a small slit in the curtains of the bay window that looked down onto to Baker Street. A rough looking chap met Dr. Romanescu on the pavement and they chatted for a moment before both climbing into a waiting carriage.

"Holmes," I said, "I suspect that you most likely made yourself an enemy, and not a friend."

"And I suspect that you are correct, my good doctor. With luck an angry enemy irrespective of his outward demeanor."

"Are you not worried that he will visit you with some violence?"

"By himself, no, though he may likely, in anger, send one of his paid ruffians after me. It is always good to encourage a possible suspect to act in anger. They become so much more careless when doing so."

"And you suspect him? Please do not tell me that his reflection could not be seen in the mirror."

Holmes broke into a short spontaneous laugh. "Oh no, my friend, nothing of the sort. Nothing is as imaginative as jousting with a vampire. Merely, very humanly suspicions at this time. But we have far too little data at present on which to form a compelling theory. If you have the time today, I would be most grateful if, as a favor, you could accompany me in a quest for the necessary information."

"You know Holmes that you do not have to ask a favor. I would be honored and, as always, intrigued. Count me with you."

"Splendid. We shall start by your educating me on one of the necessary points. When Miss Stoner gave the name of her family's firm, I detected your body and face responding ever so slightly. You know of this enterprise I gather. Please, my friend, enlighten me."

Chapter Four
The Handsome Lieutenant

It is not often that I know more on some subject that does Sherlock Holmes, but on this occasion, I did and was pleased to respond.

"Very well then. During the past two years, the entire country has been plagued by the *Medical Miracles of Mole Valley*. The certified doctors of the nation are up in arms against it. Its so-called medicines are nothing more than snake oil and magic potions. Yet they are being sold by the boat load to the elderly, the feeble-minded, the gullible, and the superstitious."

"I believe, doctor, that you have just described the general population of Great Britain," said Holmes with a merry chuckle.

"You may well be right on that score. Instead of working through our nation's doctors and hospitals and chemists, the makers of these fraudulent products advertise them directly to the unsuspecting public, making all sorts of outlandish claims. They claim to be from secret ancient Gypsy formulae. Every intimate bodily concern would be cured, from loss of virility to irregular feminine secretions. It is entirely shameful and without merit. I have no knowledge beyond the rudimentary of their products and would never let one of them into my office."

"As, of course, you should not, my excellent doctor. My concern, however, is not with medical efficacy but with profitability. As a wise man once said, 'There is profit in stupidity.' But come now, Watson, we can continue to chat as we walk. Kindly grab your coat and hat and umbrella. The morning is cold and miserable. We have places to visit and an investigation to carry out."

I did as he had suggested and was ready to depart when there was yet another knock on the Baker Street door. Our reliable landlady preceded us and then came quickly up the stairs.

"You best take off your coats, gentlemen. I believe you will want to see this one and see him now."

Holmes looked put out, displaying just a little resentment. Once he had taken up the scent of a new case, he was single-minded in the pursuit and brooked no distraction. He frowned as he took the card from Mrs. Hudson. To my surprise, after reading it, he removed his coat and laid aside his umbrella. "Watson," he said. "We may have to delay our departure for a few minutes."

He handed me the card. The name on it was Lieutenant Peter Bennion-Bowen.

"Please, Mrs. Hudson," said Holmes. "Show the officer in."

In our doorway appeared a handsome yet haggard looking young infantry officer, dressed in the uniform of the Coldstream Guards. He was as tall as Holmes and broader in the shoulders. His golden blond hair was complemented by a blond mustache. He removed his officer's cap and nodded first to Holmes and then to me. "Mr. Sherlock Holmes," he said, "and Dr. Watson, thank you for agreeing to see me. I am most grateful."

He exuded manners and military confidence and Holmes gestured to him to enter and be seated.

"Please, Lieutenant," said Holmes. "My colleague and I were preparing to leave on an urgent matter so may I request that you forget the pleasantries about how much you and your mates in the Guards enjoy reading stories about our cases and get on immediately with whatever it is that concerns you. Kindly be brief and concise and lay before us everything, as time is of the essence."

The young man was a bit taken aback but gave a practiced smile and spoke. "You stole my thunder, sir, and I am sure I should have been prepared for that. So please let me begin by asking for your assurance that whatever I say here will never be heard beyond the bounds of this room. Will you give me that guarantee, sir?"

"You need not have asked," said Holmes. "It goes without saying."

"Thank you, sir." However, he did not immediately begin his case. I watched as he closed his eyes, further exposing the dark circles under them. He clenched his fists and then opened them. His lips were moving ever so slightly as he did so and it was obvious that he was rehearsing the information he was about to impart. He then relaxed his posture and said, "I guess I may as well just blurt it out. Sir, I have reason to believe that my mother may have committed a murder." He looked at Holmes and received no immediate reply except for a nonchalantly raised eyebrow.

"You don't say," said Holmes. "And who might she have murdered?"

"My fiancée."

"When?"

"Four weeks ago?"

"Where?"

"In the estate of Stoke Moran, just outside of Leatherhead, in Surrey."

"And why would she do such a terrible thing?"

"She was violently opposed to our marriage."

"And why would she be so convicted? Most families are quite

happy to get their second sons married off, out of the house, and off of the family payroll."

The lad paused, obviously surprised that Holmes would know his birth order, but then continued. "She felt that my fiancée was, as they say, a gold-digger, and seeking to marry far above her station in life."

"And was she? Did you feel the same way?" demanded Holmes.

"Oh no, sir. Not at all. I had fallen in love with her, had courted her honorably, and looked forward to a joyful wedding and life together as husband and wife and, Lord willing, someday a family."

Holmes glared back at the lad. "Young man," he said sharply. "I despise liars. You were being compelled to marry her because you had violated her trust, acted shamefully, dishonored your regiment and left the young woman bearing your child. Now either speak the truth or get out of here this instant."

A crimson flush took over the man's face and neck. He said nothing but he closed his eyes and clenched his fists again until they turned unnaturally white. His upper body was trembling. I thought that if the floor could have opened up and devoured him he would have wished it. When he spoke, it was in a muted tone, his shame and humiliation possessing him. "I am sorry sir. You are totally correct. That is what happened. But please, sir. I beg you. Believe me when I say that even though I have acted in an unforgivable way I assure you that I had come to love and adore her. Her name was Julia and she was unusual in many ways, but she was brilliant and incredibly beautiful and I had accepted my lot with happiness, and her death was the worst event of my life." He was fighting back tears as he spoke.

"Very well," said Holmes. "Proceed with the truth from here on. How did your mother commit this heinous act?"

"I believe that she poisoned her."

"Then why have you not gone to the police? You have had four weeks in which to act. You are screening your mother. You could be charged with concealing a crime."

"Because, up until last night, I did not have any sense of certainty as there is no firm evidence. But I have turned this matter over and over in my mind every night since Julia died. If you will permit me, sir, I have applied what I have learned from reading the stories of how you solve your cases using the science of deduction. Step by step I have eliminated all other possibilities and the only one remaining, although it is utterly devastating, is that my mother must have brought about her death."

Holmes smiled, a little condescendingly. "Please. You have my attention. Tell me how you reached your conclusion."

The young fellow relaxed a little and began his story. "I met Julia just under a year ago in the village pub. She, along with her sister, was a barmaid, but she was unlike any barmaid I or my mates had ever met before. She was shy but brilliantly learned and could match wits with any of us. She was beautiful as well, with gorgeous long dark hair and blue eyes. I fell for her and quite honestly professed my adoration. After closing hours, we would spend a few stolen minutes walking along the banks of the Mole. I suppose you could say that one thing led to another and our passion got the better of us. But we had pledged ourselves to each other and knew in our hearts that we would be forever faithful."

"Of course, you would," said Holmes. "And did one thing lead to another once? Or more?"

Again a flush of red swept into the face of the young man. "More than once," he muttered. "Truthfully, many times. We could not control ourselves. It was inevitable that she would conceive, but we were beside ourselves with passion."

"Also called foolishness," said Holmes. "Continue."

"Five months ago it had become apparent to all that she was with child and everyone knew that I was the father. It was deeply humiliating, but I had to return to Stoke and face my parents and admit to my faults. My father was quite angry with me, but my mother was beyond rage. She put all the blame on Julia and took the position that she was just a local harlot who had seduced and taken advantage of her son."

"So your mother was foolish as well. You come by it honestly," said Holmes.

A spark of anger flashed in the man's weary eyes, but he then nodded and continued. "You may call it what you wish sir, but my mother has always been exceptionally fond and protective of me. I have a brother who is a decade older than I am. After I was born my mother could have no more children and so I have been her fair-haired boy, and she would hear of no possible fault in me, even though I have had many, and still do. She demanded that I abandon Julia but I refused and she became even more furious. Fortunately, my father is very level-headed and took charge and began to make arrangements for a private wedding. It was all going as well as could have been expected under such conditions when my mother, all on her own, paid a visit to our unit where we were stationed in Surrey. We were putting on a parade and march-past, and our band had come down from their quarters in Windsor to participate and all of Leatherhead was invited to come and watch. My mother heard about this event and arrived unannounced, claiming that her interest was in watching me and my fellow guards."

"Keep going," said Holmes.

"After the parade, she arranged to meet with Julia at the local inn and have tea. She said that if a barmaid were to become her daughter-in-law and mother of her grandchildren she may as well get to know her and try to start to train her to act like a lady. They met and chatted for several hours that afternoon. At supper time, I met with my mother and then escorted her to the train station. She was all smiles and said that she had become somewhat better disposed toward Julia and claimed to have lost her anger. That evening Julia and I were guests for supper at the home of Mr. and Mrs. Matthias. We were joyful with the news of my mother's coming around, and after leaving, we danced in the moonlight before I returned to my barracks and she to her family's estate house."

Here he stopped speaking.

"Continue," said Holmes.

"That was the night that she died. She was walking home and

was suddenly stricken and died in her house within the hour."

"It can happen," said Holmes. "A weak heart or a frail constitution have been known to lead to death during the period of pregnancy."

"Sir, Julia, was a country girl. She was, well, you could say she was as healthy as a horse. Please, sir, do not ask me for intimate details but I assure you that she was strong and vigorous and had exceptional endurance. Her heart was not frail, not in the least."

"And so you, Lieutenant Peter, have concluded that while having a chat your mother put poison into your fiancée's tea and murdered her. Is that it?"

"Why, yes sir. That is the conclusion I reached. I have fought against it in my mind for four weeks now. But last night I admitted that it was the only possible explanation, horrible though it is."

"And is there any other evidence?"

"Last weekend I had leave to return to my family's home in Stoke-on-Trent. While in the garage looking at a new set of engines and batteries I discovered a bottle of arsenic. It was clearly labeled and was less than half full. My mother could easily have taken it with her and poisoned Julia's tea and thus murdered her. It is the only possible explanation for her death. Therefore, sir, it must be the truth."

Holmes nodded sagely and then smiled at the young officer. "You have used the processes of logic and deduction well, indeed. Permit me to inquire about a matter that is beyond the realm of science, though. Was there any hint of anything supernatural in your interaction with Miss Julia? Not in actual factual occurrences, but in your conversations?"

"I am sorry sir. I fail to understand. What aspect of the supernatural are you referring to?"

"Allow me to be explicit, and know only that I have my reasons for asking. Did Miss Julia believe in vampires?"

Again a blush came over the young man's face. He looked at Holmes in disbelief.

"I had read that you had powers of perception that were beyond all possible explanations and I should have expected your question, but it is an area that is exceptionally private and intimate between Julia and me and I hesitate to betray her trust and answer."

"I do not wish to be harsh," said Holmes, "but might I remind you that Julia is no more and I assure you that she will not now object to anything that might help me solve the mystery of her death. Please just answer the question and know that whatever you say will never become known to anyone other than Dr. Watson and me. Your answer, young man."

He spoke in a near whisper. "Julia did hold a peculiar belief in vampires, sir. That is the truth. It must have been the result of her having been taught by her governesses and the Gypsies. She believed that the story of Count Dracula was fact and history and not just fictional nonsense. Her belief, sir, was beyond merely knowing that they existed. She was quite fascinated by them."

"In what way? Please be explicit. My time is pressed."

He stared at the floor and continued to whisper. "During those times when we were intimate, she would pretend to be a Gypsy girl and insist on my pretending to be a vampire and making her look intently into my eyes, and then biting her on her neck, and on her breast. I was told that her dying words were that a vampire had taken her life. Now please sir, this is all quite humiliating. Must you insist on asking me about my private life? I came here because of my conclusions about my mother, and that was painful enough for me to speak of. Must you further embarrass me by demanding the details of my intimate life with a young woman who is now dead?"

Holmes sat back in his chair. "Quite right you are, Lieutenant. I have heard enough. I will accept your case, young man and as I have no interest in the acquirement of wealth, I will, as is my habit, set no fee until I have solved it. I suggest that you go now and get back to your unit. If you hurry, you can catch a morning train at Waterloo. I will be in contact with you, but it may not be for several weeks. Meanwhile, I assure you that I will proceed in complete confidence, and I suggest that you put your mind at ease and attend to your duties with the Guards. Now, if you will please excuse us, we have other matters that are demanding our attention and I must ask you to be on your way."

Lieutenant Bennion-Bowen rose and departed, casting a very fearful glance back at Sherlock Holmes as he passed through our door.

I smiled and addressed my colleague. "Very well then, Holmes. We have now been visited by a young woman who believes in vampires, a quack of a doctor who does not, and an infantry officer who pretends to be one. What is next? And where are we off to this morning?"

"To learn all about vampires," he replied.

"And how are we going to do that, seeing as we are in London and not Transylvania?"

"By going and chatting with the expert."

"You don't say," I offered. "Some ossified folklore professor in Cambridge, perhaps?"

"Not at all. We are going to have a chat with Mr. Stoker since he bears much of the responsibility for some of the recent sightings of vampires in London; recent bitings as well no doubt. Half of the untimely deaths in this past year have been attributed in the penny press to vampires all because of Mr. Stoker. I recall that he is friendly with your literary agent, that fellow Doyle. Would that connection be enough to gain us an interview?"

"I would think so. Give me a moment and I will dash off a note and find a page to run it over to the Lyceum Theater."

Mr. Bram Stoker had become notorious in the past six months for his scandalous and sensational book — a work of fiction in case you were wondering — about Count Dracula and the expedition to the haunted castle in Transylvania. When he was not stirring the blood, so to speak, of the English reading public, he worked as the very successful manager of the Lyceum Theater and its famous principle actor, Henry Irving. He and my agent, Art Doyle, were friends and as a fellow writer, I was quite sure he would accept to see me, especially if I were to bring along the most famous detective in London. I scribbled a note asking for a meeting that morning and on Baker Street found a page-boy on a bicycle who sped away towards the Strand.

We donned our Aquascutums and our hats, and took our umbrellas in hand and departed 221B Baker Street.

We donned our Aquascutums and our hats, and took our umbrellas in hand and departed 221B Baker Street.

Chapter Five
The Vampire Expert and the Inspector

"Gentlemen, I am honored to meet you," said a beaming Mr. Abraham Stoker. "Such a delight to receive your note and, of course, I am free to meet with you. This is the theater and mornings are always open while our actors and stage workers recover from the triumph or disaster of the previous evening. So welcome. Do come in."

Bram Stoker's office was attached to the front office of the Lyceum Theater. On the walls were countless photographs of the rich and famous as well as the celebrated and infamous, all taken as they entered the theater, and many standing beside a beaming Mr. Henry Irving, the owner of the Lyceum and the finest actor in the West End. There were even photographs of him along with Mr.

Stoker in America, and I recognized the chap beside them as the President of the United States.

"I am intrigued," Stoker continued. "If Mr. Holmes and Dr. Watson come to call then there must be some mystery behind their doing so. It cannot possibly be about scandalous infidelities amongst the acting crowd, or even embezzlements of box office receipts, for those are a dime a dozen and hardly worth a write-up in the penny press, let alone a story in *The Strand*. And I rather doubt that Sherlock Holmes is investigating something so unscientific as vampires. So do tell, gentleman, to what do I owe this honor?"

"You hit the ball on your second swing," said Holmes. "We are here with regards to vampires."

Bram Stoker first looked surprised and then broke into a friendly laugh. "Well then, you have come to the right place. I have become, it seems, the reigning expert on that topic in all of London. Please, gentlemen, be seated. Brandy? Of course not, it is still before noon. Then a cigar, perhaps? I have some unusual ones that are imported from the Carpathians. Mind you, one can never be sure if the scent will not summon the un-dead back from the grave." He laughed again as he opened his humidor and offered us some fine-looking but musky smelling tobacco. Holmes accepted and lit up. I declined.

"So," he continued, beaming at us, "can it be true that Sherlock Holmes is investigating a crime by a vampire? How splendid. I do hope that this crime will be written up, Dr. Watson. It will do wonders for the sales of my book."

"I believe," I said in response, "that your book has already sold untold numbers of copies and if only you had made some reference to Sherlock Holmes therein, it is we who would have benefited."

"I promise you, sirs, that should I ever write another story about vampires, that you will both be principal characters. The twists and turns of the plot of such a story would be fascinating."

"Yes," said Holmes, "indeed they would. However, sir, we are here to ask about matters concerning a crime, a murder most likely, in which your vampires appear to have had a role, and we are in need of further information."

"Then ask away. I promise I will not bite back," Stoker said, again with a guffaw of pleasant laughter.

Holmes offered a thin-lipped smile in return.

"I assume, Mr. Stoker that you conducted extensive research in preparation for your most unusual book."

"Over two years of mornings in the reading room of the British Museum; off and on of course, between tours with our theater company. I read everything I could find on the topic."

"Excellent. So tell me: are there such things as bats that suck blood from their prey? Are there any such thing as vampire bats?"

"Most certainly there are. I read several accounts from highly esteemed biologists on exactly that topic." He gave an exaggerated theatrical nod and did not attempt to conceal the twinkle in his eye.

"I will make my question more precise," acknowledged Holmes. "Has such a species ever been sighted in Britain or on the Continent?"

"Most certainly they have not. They have only ever been found in the upper reaches of the Amazon jungle. They are rather discriminating when it comes to climate and our miserable British weather is not to their liking. And the winters on the Continent are just a bit too chilly for them."

"Ah yes," said Holmes. "Good to know. And is there any report of their attacking humans, and if so, have they ever been deadly?"

"Most certainly on both counts," said Stoker, now barely concealing his laughter. "And let me spare you the next question. There are two reports in the literature of vampire bats in South America having become rabid and biting children, who, not able to get appropriate medical attention, succumbed to their affliction and died. But no, there are no reports of anyone's having become a member of the un-dead for eternity. All reports otherwise are the stuff of wild imaginations, including, I confess, my own."

"Then how in heaven's name," asked Holmes, "did you come up

with your tale? And why on earth would you undertake to write such a ghoulish account?"

"Oh, my good man. Why do we stage plays that have witches in Scotland plotting with eye of newt and toe of frog? For the money, my dear man, for the money. The first rule of theater is you must give the audience what they want, and heaven knows they want their spines tingled. How many copies of a book telling the journey to Transylvania of a geologist looking for fossils would I have sold? Instead, I wrote something that created endless letters to the editor, mostly condemning me, and with every new accusation of scandal and impropriety, I sold more books. There is no magic, sir. It is the stuff of the business of theater."

"Indeed, it is," acknowledged Holmes. "I had not read your book until a few hours ago, so forgive me if I am not well-versed on the content. There was one thing that puzzled me, however."

"And what was that?"

"All of the victims of your vampire were young virgins. If vampires truly are evil incarnate, why the preference for virgins?"

"An astute observation, Mr. Holmes. The truth is, at least according to the ancient Gypsy legends and Romanian folklore, that vampires had no use for virgins. Their preference, being aligned with the devil as they were, was for those who had lost their innocence. There are some quite ribald tales of their attacking their victims in the very act of illicit coitus. But that would have been a step too far for the English reading public. I have had the Legion of Public Decency chasing me as it is. No publisher would have dared touch the legends verbatim. So I had to settle for virgins. Mind you, in my next tale, along with Sherlock Holmes and Dr. Watson hunting down vampire earls and duchesses, I might just add something more in keeping with the source material." He laughed loudly and I have to confess that Holmes and I chuckled along with him.

"I am not sure that I would look forward to that edition," I said.

"My good doctor, I would share the royalties," said Stoker.

We paused as Holmes took a slow draft on his Carpathian cigar.

Then he spoke in a serious tone. "It is all well and good to amuse ourselves at the expense of the reading and theater-going public, but my concern is about a crime that took place in the corporeal world. Have you, sir, had any information given back to you about crimes that may have been committed in which the criminal made use of the fear of vampires?"

Mr. Stoker removed the smile from his face. "With regret, sir, yes I have. More than one. Mind you the world of the theater is overflowing with rumors of all sorts and one can never hope to know which are true and which are wholly fanciful. Most are the latter. But yes sir, just this past month it was reported to me that a young woman in Surrey had died and claimed in her dying words to have been the victim of a vampire.

"This past spring there were two other stories, and the previous fall two more. All had vampires attacking young women who were gravid and expecting to deliver a child within the next month or so. I heard several versions of these stories, all with differing details. The events were said to have taken place in Wales and the Lake District and goodness knows where else, but most of the accounts, other than Surrey, had them up north somewhere. I could say that I had no time to ask for any more information, but the truth is I did not want to know. I am sure you can understand my motives."

"Yes, sir. Unlike your vampires, you are all too human, as are we all," said Holmes. With that, he concluded the conversation and we departed. Standing out on Wellington Street I turned to him, "It appears you have stumbled into something, Holmes. These vampires are not just a one-night performance. They have been on tour for the past year or two. So Mr. Holmes, where to now?"

"I shall have to do something that I am loathe to do," he replied. "I shall have to seek the help of Inspector Lestrade."

Sherlock Holmes and Scotland Yard were not on friendly terms. Nevertheless, a grudging respect between them had developed over the years and they were known on occasion to acknowledge each other's strengths. Holmes admitted that their detectives could do determined, plodding and detailed digging when necessary, and their inspectors admitted that the unorthodox consulting detective had made leaps of intuition and logic that led to the solving of crimes that had had them utterly befuddled.

And so it was that we took a cab to The Embankment and found ourselves knocking on a door bearing the name of G. Lestrade, Inspector. It opened and the familiar sallow, rat-faced, dark-eyed officer of The Yard appeared in front of us.

Without so much as a "hello" Lestrade began. "The note from the front desk said you were here seeking information and advice from Scotland Yard. I'll believe that one when hell freezes over. You and I only have anything to do with each other when I am at my wits end and so desperate that I call upon you and those methods of yours which we are not permitted to use. So the truth now Holmes... what do you want?"

"While it may be humbling, indeed humiliating Inspector," said Holmes with an ingratiating nod, "the truth is that I am working on a case and require some more information, and need it quite urgently. And I have to confess that your good office is the most logical place to begin. May we enter and seek your assistance?"

Lestrade looked positively smacked in the face with a codfish. "Very well. This is a surprise. Come in. Sit down."

Once we were seated in the Spartan but cluttered office and Lestrade had pushed aside the teacups that littered his desk, Holmes began.

"Inspector, my question is serious, I assure you, even if it it sounds nonsensical. Do you have any information concerning sudden deaths of young women in the past two years in which a vampire was a factor?"

I had expected Lestrade to break out in a mocking laugh. Instead, he just fixed his gimlet eye on Holmes and said nothing. Then, using only the soles of his feet for propulsion, he turned his wheeled chair one hundred and eighty degrees and waddled it to the credenza behind his desk. He leaned forward and picked up the fifth

46

stack of files from the left and spun and waddled back. He reached his arms out and dropped the files in front of Holmes.

"If I were a superstitious imbecile I would have to say that you are in league with the devil and his vampires, Holmes. So, yes, these files came in last week. All unnatural deaths in Britain have to be reported to us through the Office of the Chief Coroner. A young recruit who has the job of reading them somehow recalled that several of the hundreds of files he had read over the past two years had a vampire flying around, and he went back through the boxes of cases and pulled these six out and sent them up to us. You can take them to the refectory to read and then leave them at the front desk. Gregson took a look at them and said that there was something strange happening, but I will confess that we have nothing to go on. So go and do your deducing and more power to you." He stood and opened the door of his office, saying without words that he wanted us gone. Holmes picked up the files and we made our way to the refectory in the basement of New Scotland Yard.

We took ourselves to the far corner of the room and sat down. Holmes lit up his pipe, opened the first file and burst out in laughter. He handed it over to me. On the top of the pages was a hand-written note that ran:

Lestrade:

These are beyond queer.

Suggest you give them to S.H.

Gregson.

"How delightful to know that they are reduced to sending me their queerest cases," said Holmes, looking quite smug.

"I believe, my friend," I admonished, "that you would be better to leave your gloating until you have caught your vampire and driven a stake through his heart."

"Right you are," he responded. He then divided the files between us and for the entire rest of the afternoon we read them. I had to admit that I have nowhere near the amazing memory of Sherlock Holmes and had to make copious notes in order to keep the reports straight in my mind. They had been compiled by the local police officers and coroners and were completely unorganized in their presentation. Nevertheless, I noted a few matters that struck me as possibly having significance.

The clock had struck four when Holmes put down the final file and looked across the table at me. "Very well, then, Watson. What insights have you acquired by the study of the data?"

I have expected this question and, frankly, I did not like having it posed to me. No matter what I offered, it was always too obvious and far short of what Holmes was able to observe. Invariably I felt like a blockhead. Nevertheless, I gave it a good try.

"Other than the incident of Miss Julia in Surrey, all of the cases are in the Lake District and Snowdonia."

"Excellent observation Watson. Of course, Gregson had that marked on the first page of the file. What else?"

Here we go again, I thought to myself. "Very well then. All took place at quite secluded private institutions operated by charities that take in young fallen women until their offspring are born. Our vampires have very specific preferences. Quite discriminating tastes one might say." I smiled at my wit. Holmes did not.

"Keep going."

"The reports of the local police all refer to a claim by the victims that they were attacked by a bat. The medical reports all confirm that the women died quite quickly and that they had small wounds, consistent with a bite from a bat, on their necks or breasts or both. Some concluded that since no bat could inflict a deadly bite, they must have died of heart failure brought on by fright."

"Yes, those were common factors in the reports. You have failed however to observe the curious coincidence of the dates of the events."

"Oh. Was I supposed to note that they all took place on the night of the full moon when vampires emerge to do their evil business?"

"As a matter of fact, yes. There had been a full moon either on the date or close to it of each of the events recorded. That is significant but not the most telling detail."

"And what would that be, Holmes?"

"Are you aware of any such trade union known as the International Brotherhood of Vampires? Hmm, are you?" He raised his eyebrows and affected a supercilious look.

"Please Holmes, circumlocution is not necessary."

"Our vampires only work on Saturday evenings. Not a single event took place during the week and they honored the Sabbath and refrained from laboring thereon. Their efforts were all confined to the late evening hours of a Saturday. Now I am quite sure that any species of bat is quite unaware of the days of the week and would be out looking for prey regardless of the calendar. Is that not so, my good doctor?"

"It is most peculiar behavior for bats but, of course, not for humans."

"Precisely. But which humans?"

"I would suppose that, if nothing else, we can eliminate the angry mother-in-law as a suspect. She has only one second son and unless he has been priaptically prolific, I do not believe that any of these victims were even known to him. She most certainly did not go out to the woods and poison five other young mothers-to-be on Saturday evenings in which bats were flying about."

Holmes said nothing for a few moments as he pondered my conclusion.

"The balance of probabilities is certainly weighing in the direction you have said, but it is not yet entirely conclusive. Neither the mother-in-law nor the band of Gypsies fit with the other cases.

Their location was an exception and took place months later. We have the testimony of her son while given under duress, that his mother is a woman of profound determination and becomes an irresistible force when set on her chosen path. He did not use the word "ruthless", but it was not far from his lips. So yes, while it is unlikely, we cannot altogether remove the lady yet. Further investigation is needed."

"Quite so, Holmes. And where now are we off to?"

"I would normally suggest that we move in haste as we appear to be dealing with a most peculiar killer or killers. However, they only work on Saturdays and Saturday night has already passed, and by this coming Saturday so will the full moon. I suspect that we have three weeks and few days in which to carry out a thorough investigation. Would you mind taking a short trip up to the Lake District, preceded by a visit to an angry lady in Staffordshire on the way?"

"Not at all. The early autumn is supposed to be a splendid time up north. I shall look forward to it."

"Excellent. Then let us return these files to the inspector and find supper and a good night's sleep back on Baker Street."

"Might I remind you Holmes that we still have a young woman at Baker Street and we must find her a safe place to stay. We cannot impose unreasonably on Mrs. Hudson."

"You are, in your always considerate way, entirely correct, although I have no idea what to do with the girl. I shall give that some thought on the way home.

Chapter Six
The Angry Mother-in-Law

By the time a cab had dropped us off at Baker Street, Sherlock Holmes had still not arrived at a decision with regards to Miss Helen Stoner. We inquired of Mrs. Hudson concerning her as soon as we entered.

"She's up and gone. Left near two hours ago," Mrs. Hudson informed us.

"Good heavens," said Holmes, quite alarmed. "Where did she go?"

"She was awake and bathed and dressed by ten o'clock and first ran off to the telegraph office, saying that she had to send a note to her fiancé. Then about four hours later, a lady named Mrs. Armitage, who I gather, is about to be the young woman's mother-in-law, came knocking on the door and said she was there to fetch her and take her over to Reading."

"Good Lord," I gasped, "not a second enraged mother-in-law to deal with."

"This women," said Holmes. "was she angry? Did she speak in derogatory terms to Miss Stoner?"

"Oh, she was derogatory, all right. Downright bubbling over with nasty words. But not one of them towards Miss Stoner. Oh, no, Mr. Holmes. She was quite pleasant to the girl but called her son every name in the book. It was really a bit amusing it was. Miss Stoner was left trying to put in a good word for her future husband and the mother was having none of it."

"Ah, that is a relief to hear," said Holmes.

"Well now, that is a strange thing to say, I do say, Mr. Holmes," returned Mrs. Hudson. "A relief, you say. I would say it was passing strange. Most mothers adore their sons, but not this one. She went so far as to call him a "horny little blighter, a bloody young billy goat, just like his father was." She was quite solicitous to Miss Stoner and I brought them a cup of tea and they chatted here for near an hour before leaving. Now I don't make it a habit to eavesdrop on anyone you know, gentlemen, and most certainly not on any of your clients, Mr. Holmes, but the two of them were sitting right in my parlor, not upstairs in your rooms and so it could not be avoided. Mrs. Armitage, in quite a kindly way, quizzed the young woman, and within a few minutes seemed to have taken to her, sir. And then didn't she go ahead and ask Miss Stoner outright if she had been a virgin before meeting her son, and Miss Stoner assured her that she had. And then didn't Mrs. Armitage call her son no end of awful names, most of which I would never say myself. Now, I couldn't say for certain, Mr. Holmes, not being a detective as you are, but to my mind, I suspect that Mrs. Armitage had gone through a similar experience herself with the man who is now her husband and her sympathies were for certain with Miss Stoner.

"When tea was done she took the girl by the arm and said that they were going off to the shops and then back to Reading on a late train. That was about an hour ago. I didn't try to discourage them sir, but I did insist that they use the back door to leave. I hope that you are not upset with me. But if a young girl is not safe with a mother-in-law who is set on looking after her then I don't know who is."

For the first time since he had awakened me in the middle of the night, Holmes's face had a look of relief on it. He thanked Mrs. Hudson and graciously asked her to prepare our supper and then walked slowly to the mantle and removed one of our decanters. "A bit of brandy before we eat? What say, Watson?"

As soon as supper had been cleared away Holmes rose and moved from the table to his armchair and lit his pipe. "I have some contemplation required of me, Watson. So forgive me for ignoring you for the rest of the evening. Could we meet tomorrow morning at Paddington? At eleven o'clock? If you get there before I do would you mind finding us a couple of seats to Stoke-on-Trent? Not that I think we will need it, but you might bring your service revolver along."

He did not wait for an answer and closed his eyes and entered his world of contemplation. I retired to my room with a copy of Cooks' guide to holiday spots in England. A journey to the Lake District, however short, would be a lovely treat in autumn and give zest to our investigations.

I rose the following morning at what I thought to be a good hour only to find that Holmes was up and gone already from our rooms. Having learned to travel light while in the medical corps, I packed up a small overnight bag, taking care to slide my Eley's No. 2 along with my toothbrush between the folds of my pajamas. It was a brisk clear morning and I enjoyed the walk down Baker Street and along Marylebone Road until I reached the Paddington Basin and Station. Trains for Stoke-on-Trent left every hour, with the next one due to depart at 11:10 am. I secured us two tickets, both one-way, assuming that we would be returning directly from the lakes.

At precisely fifty-nine minutes past ten o'clock, Sherlock Holmes appeared on the platform. He had been hurrying and was all huffing and puffing as he approached me.

"At ease, my friend," I announced. "You have ten minutes to spare. But do tell what you were doing up to so early on a fine September morning?"

"I have been first to Westminster and then to the Doctors' Commons. A bit of a hike, you know, from Knightrider all the way to Paddington. I thought the walk would give me time to think, but I had to hurry to make it here. Rest assured, I will show you what I have discovered."

Once in the train cabin and on our way, Holmes produced a sheet of blue paper, all covered with notes and figures.

"As they say, Watson, where there is a will there is not only a way but a war between relatives. Surviving wives, sons, daughters, grandchildren and other issues legitimate and otherwise can be moved to desperate and ruthless measures."

"Ah, so you have been reading wills. Doing the old *cui bono* trek, have you?"

"Indeed, I have. It would appear that both the angry Mrs. Bennion-Bowen and the obsequious Dr. Romanescu had strong pecuniary interests in intervening in the marriages and child-bearing of Miss Julia Stoner."

"How strong?"

"Mrs. Bennion-Bowen would have lost a full two-thirds of her estate's yearly income, leaving her with far too little to continue to live in the manner to which she has become accustomed."

"And the humble country doctor?"

"He would have nothing. Mr. Stoner, the long-departed diplomat, left the property and all of the shares in the medical firm only in trust to his wife, and then, upon her passing, to be divided between his daughters upon their marriages or upon their reaching the age of twenty-one. The firm had, as Miss Stoner told us, very little income until recently. Under the clever direction of the Romanian, it has become exceptionally prosperous, most likely as a result of the selling of its snake oils to the gullible public. While he may have had the power to change the products that are made and sold, the shares remain in the estate trust of the late husband and were bequeathed to his daughters."

"And what about the local Gypsies, what did they have to gain?"

Holmes shrugged. "That I do not know. It is possible that they were merely acting as assassins paid by the doctor. They remain somewhat under suspicion, but their world is impossible for an outsider to penetrate."

"But now we are on our way to confront the young lieutenant's mother. The angry one. Correct?" I asked.

"Correct," affirmed Holmes.

"And pray tell just how you plan to do that. Even her fair-haired boy seemed to think that she was a bit of a tigress."

"So he did, and from now until we knock on a door just outside of Stoke-on-Trent, I shall be contemplating my strategy."

For the rest of the journey, Holmes did exactly that. His eyes were closed and his hands folded in his lap. I could detect his lips moving as he rehearsed the interview with the fearsome lady. Every so often he would shake his head, erase the most recent draft of his imagined script, and start over.

The Bennion-Bowen family was not without means, as was obvious by the location of their pleasant home in the Caverswall village at the edge of the city. The mid-sized but still stately home sat at the end of a long, oak-lined laneway. Our cab was met by an attentive stable boy who stopped the horse and inquired as to our names. An involuntary grin appeared on his face when he was told that he was looking at the famous detective, Sherlock Holmes, and the chap who wrote up the stories of his escapades. As a well-trained member of the help, however, he made no comment beyond asking us to follow him to the door. A maid greeted us, led us into a comfortable and sunny front room, and offered us tea.

Two minutes later the tea arrived, and a minute after that a woman appeared in the doorway. She was almost as tall as Holmes and remarkably slender. Her blonde hair, accented by a few strands of silver, was pulled back into a tight bun. She was dressed in gleaming riding boots, jodhpurs that outlined her muscular lower body, and a tailored riding jacket. Under her arm, she carried a riding crop and her gloves. These she placed on a side table as she approached Holmes and me.

"This is indeed an unusual surprise. Having England's most famous detective visit Caverswall could never have been imagined. Let me guess, Mr. Holmes. You are here to prevent the murder of our Bishop. I believe I could list off a hundred members of this diocese who would happily do him in." She laughed in a brittle and sharp manner and then went on. "I am Mrs. Faulkner Bennion-Bowen, so please tell me what Mr. Sherlock Holmes is doing in my parlor."

She did not ask us to be seated and she remained standing.

"Since I assume you have little patience for beating about the bushes," began Holmes. He got no further before she replied.

"Excellent deduction, Sherlock Holmes, now proceed precisely and concisely."

Homes gave a polite nod and continued. "I have no interest in the forthcoming demise of your bishop, but I am interested in the untimely death a month ago of a young woman who was about to become your daughter-in-law."

She stared at Holmes and he met her eyeball to eyeball. "About bloody time someone started to ask questions," she said. "The local police and medics were complete imbeciles. Healthy young women, especially rough country girls, do not up and die from fright of seeing a bat, and the idiots who went on about vampires should all be in Broadmoor." Here she stopped and gestured for us to be seated. She sat in the couch across from us.

"Very well then, Mr. Holmes. I am rather pleased that you have taken an interest in Miss Stoner's death. How may I assist you?"

"I am informed that you met with Miss Stoner in the village inn during the afternoon of her death."

The lady said nothing for several seconds, and then let out yet another sharp laugh. "Oh my, am I a suspect? Of all the things I have accused of in my life, and they have been many, murdering young women has not yet been one of them. Oh my, this has become interesting Mr. Holmes. Let me see. Did I have the motive, the means, and the opportunity? All three have to be present do they not? That's what is written in all the mystery stories. Hmm. I suppose I did. Shall I describe them to you, sir? And Dr. Watson, I do hope you will be taking notes. How deliciously famous I could become if I were to be written up in one of your stories." She laughed yet again.

"Let me help you out. Did I have a motive? Why yes, two of them. Either one would do. Take your pick. I would have immediately lost most of my income from the estate, and if that were not enough, there is the belief held by all men that mothers are desperate to have their sons marry up and a barmaid is truly a long way in the opposite direction. Are you getting this Dr. Watson? As for the opportunity, I could, of course, have poisoned the poor thing as she sipped on her tea in the inn. And as to the means, well I suppose that there is always arsenic lying around. So there you go, Mr. Holmes. I have solved your case for you." One more time she laughed.

"Thank you, madam," said Holmes. "Now having carried that part of my investigation for me would you mind completing my work and giving me the reasons for refuting the evidence you have offered? That is also part of my task."

"And do I receive a portion of the fee? Most likely not, but I suspect it is a pittance and hardly worth the time. Very well then, I shall serve both as prosecutor and defense. The money is meaningless. I am blessed with a very generous income of my own from my family and the part I would lose from the estate amounts to less than a tenth of what I now receive. As you are supposed to be a detective, sir, I am sure you are capable of confirming that by looking into the public records. As to poisoning the girl's tea with arsenic, I do believe, and if you are the expert on poisoning as I read that you are, then you may correct me, but enough arsenic to cause a healthy young woman to die within hours would have to fill a teacup to overflowing. There would be no room for the tea, and even a poorly bred country girl could tell the difference from the smell if not from the first taste."

"You are correct," said Holmes, coolly. "Of course, there are poisons that are more concentrated."

"For which I would have had to acquire, which is against the law as they are highly controlled. And even a few drops would be enough to curdle the milk in the tea and render it undrinkable, except perhaps for Americans." Again she voiced her forced and bitter laugh.

"You did not address the other motive," said Holmes. "You were, I have been told, furiously opposed to the marriage. Such passion has been enough in other cases."

She gave Holmes another hard look. "I don't suppose you would reveal who it was who so told you? No... of course not. I have not an enemy in the world who would speak ill of me, at least not beyond the three or four score that come to mind. So yes, Mr. Holmes, I was enraged beyond words when I first heard that a local prostitute had entrapped my son and was about to become a member of my family. I was livid and did everything I could to prevent it."

"Which you failed to do, and so you went and met with her."

"I did exactly that. My son's unit is due to be sent overseas in the next few weeks. I would have been saddled with a barmaid and a screaming brat living under my roof and I was determined to meet with her and lay down the rules of the house before she so much as stepped off the train platform at Stoke-on-Trent."

"And is that what happened?" pressed Holmes.

At this point, the lady did not say anything. She got up and walked over to the tea caddy and poured herself a cup, stirred it and came back, sat down and took a slow sip.

"No, Mr. Holmes that was not what happened."

"Please madam."

"It was not what happened at all. The first thing that happened was that I was absolutely struck dumb with the appearance of the girl. I had expected a hard-faced wench with wretched teeth. And instead, I found myself looking at an angelic face of intoxicating beauty. I knew then and there that my son, at least, had a discerning eye."

"Yes. And then?"

"I began to interrogate her. I had planned to be tough on her, but her smile and eyes dashed those thoughts away. I asked her about many things and was utterly stunned to hear her respond. She was quite smart, very informed, and positively eloquent. Frankly, she is a whole lot brighter than my son. At least, on an intellectual level, he would have been marrying up and I hoped she would not find him to be insufferably dull. And then it turned out that her father was from a good family and had had a promising career in the Foreign Office before his untimely death on the Continent."

"And as a result of her intelligence, wit, and good breeding you changed your plans?"

For the first time since we arrived, Mrs. Bennion-Bowen smiled, folded her arms across her chest and sat back in her chair. "I will confess that something even more unsuspected happened to me. I looked at this beautiful young thing in front of me, and fixed my gaze at her lovely rounded tummy, and I knew that inside her she was carrying my first grandchild. I was caught quite off-guard as I had read that there is a part of a woman's brain that turns to complete irrational mush when she learns that she is about to become a grandmother, and had denied that I would ever succumb to such nonsense … but I did."

Here she stopped and took another slow sip of tea. "I know you may find it hard to believe, Mr. Holmes, but the news of her death and the loss of my grandchild ripped into my heart, again without warning, like nothing I have ever known."

I could see a tear forming in the corner of her eye. She dabbed it with her handkerchief.

"My older son has shown no interest in marriage, and Peter is so distraught and grief stricken that he may never love another. Perhaps I am being foolish but fear I will never again be blessed with the prospect of a grandchild. I have forced myself to believe that Providence had acted and that the local officials who did the investigation must have been correct even if I thought them incompetent. I have told myself that, Lord willing, I will be reunited with them in heaven if I can bully St. Peter into letting me in."

In the same manner as her son had done in our presence the day before, she then closed her eyes and clenched her fists until her fingers had lost all natural color.

"Your presence in my house, Mr. Holmes, tells me that you do not believe that Julia died of fright from seeing a bat and that you suspect foul play. So let me assure you of one more thing, sir." She sat forward as she spoke. "If the young woman who was about to be the mother of my grandson or granddaughter was the victim of a murderer, then, believe me, sir, I would not hesitate to murder whoever did that. And I would not waste my time with something so painless as poison. I would personally cut the bastard's throat. You may tell Scotland Yard I said so." Her face was flushed and her entire body was trembling. I could not know what Holmes was thinking, but I did not doubt that she would do exactly what she had said.

Holmes nodded toward her and rose from his chair. I followed suit and we bid the lady good-bye.

Chapter Seven
To the Lake District

The trap we had hired was waiting for us and we left Cavenswall and returned to the train station.

"My good doctor," said Holmes. "I request your learned medical opinion."

"By all means, ask anything."

"Is it a fact of modern medicine that a woman of a certain age, on learning that she is about to become a grandmother, experiences the turning to mush of a certain portion of her brain?"

"To borrow the words of the Lady Jane, it is a truth universally acknowledged. And may I assume that the lady of mushy-brain has now been struck off the list of suspects."

"A theory pointing toward her certainly presents some difficulties. However, I have learned, the hard way at times, that as a professional detective I have no choice but to run down every detail of every case before making a final conclusion. So, duty bound, I will check the facts on the lady's financial situation. However, for now, I acknowledge that my attention has been directed primarily toward the Lake District, and only secondarily to the mother-in-law or the Gypsies."

"You know, Holmes," I added before he disappeared into his contemplative state. "You never did say why you contacted Westminster. I assume that you were seeking information from your brother Mycroft. Would I be correct?"

"Indeed, you are. Even beyond his exceptional memory he has access to every file of the British government both at home and abroad. So I asked him for a report on the death over a decade ago of a Mr. Stoner of the Foreign Office while posted to Romania."

"I assume that he reported back."

"He did. The report on file said that Mr. Stoner had been serving as the First Secretary - Political at the Embassy and had been highly regarded. He made a journey for personal reasons across Transylvania and to the regional city of Cluj-Napoca. The hotel staff found him dead in his bed the morning after he arrived. An officer from the Embassy went there post haste but could learn nothing. The hotel staff said, to a person, that they were certain that he had been attacked by a vampire, having been so foolish as to leave his balcony windows open during the night of a full moon. The doctor who examined him recorded it as heart failure."

"So you have concluded that he must have had a heart attack since I trust you are not entertaining thoughts of vampires."

"The name of the examining medical officer on the death certificate was a Dr. Grigore Romanescu. So I hate to disappoint you, my dear friend, but I am indeed considering the possibility of vampires."

It was not a long train journey from Stoke-on-Trent to the Lake District and the train passed through some of the most pleasant countryside in England. The inter-city train took us all the way to Kendal, where we caught the narrow gauge into the village of

Windermere. Holmes, who I concluded, had somehow managed to travel through every county in Great Britain, had been here before but it was my very first visit and I was enraptured with the natural beauty. I had, while on leave from my service in Afghanistan, stayed briefly at the renowned Windermere Hotel in Darjeeling, which had been named in honor of the lovely Lake Windermere that now sparkled before me in the late afternoon sun. The Himalayas were far greater in all aspects than the peaks of the Lake District, but to my mind could not match the feelings of calm and tranquility that this loveliest of all parts of England gave to the soul of the observer.

As I stood looking out over the lake I began to recite Wordsworth:

I wandered lonely as a cloud
That floats on high o'er vales and hills …

That was as far as I could go before the acutely unsentimental Sherlock Holmes interrupted me.

"Daffodils are dead and gone for the season. So come, Watson, say good-bye to Willie the Weep. We have to secure lodgings for the night so that at first light we can go and find one of the homes where expectant young women are attacked by vampires."

Not far from the station was the other famous Windermere Hotel. The manager, a friendly young chap named Giles, arranged for a dogcart to be at our use the next morning.

"The institution," said Giles, "that you are looking for is named the Mary and Martha Home. There are several of these homes in the district for un-wed mothers. Yours is about three miles south of the village on the road to Bowness. We do not have much contact with them. The women who run it keep mostly to themselves and the girls who are sent there are not permitted to leave the grounds. Most of our news about the place comes from husbands and wives who stay at the hotel while visiting the Home in the hope of being able to adopt one of the babies that are born there. I'll have a note sent down to them this evening letting them know of your visit. I see no reason why they would not be happy to see you."

A ride along the shore of one of the lovely bodies of water in the Lake District is truly a pleasing experience, particularly on a cold, bright fall morning when the trees and wayside hedges are bathed in the colors of early autumn. I smiled all the way from the hotel to the turnoff, just a few miles away. Holmes, on the other hand, was buried in his overcoat, his hat pulled down to his eyebrows. I offered a few pleasantries about the vistas but received no more than a grunt in reply and gave up.

We approached the gate of our destination. The pillars and ironwork looked quite recent, as did the landscaping. A young woman was waiting for us at the gate. She was still in her teens and quite obviously expecting a child. She gave us a warm smile and, upon confirming that we were indeed Sherlock Holmes and Dr. Watson, she opened the gate and directed our driver to the large manor house at the top of the hill. As we approached, I could see that the home included not just the large central house but several smaller cottages, well-manicured lawns and tended gardens, a sports field and a set of stables. It occurred to me that if a young woman were required to leave her home and spend her time of lying in at an institution then this one, at least, was far from the worst option available.

Another young woman, again well advanced in her expectancy, met us at the door. "Please gentlemen, come in," she said graciously, with an accent that I would have placed in Belgravia. "Miss Featherstone is expecting you. Please, follow me."

She led us into an elegant foyer and towards an office door. The sign on it read: *Director*. She opened it and introduced us to a secretary, who in turn opened the door to the inner office. As we entered a woman of a certain number of years, plus perhaps another ten, rose from the chair and walked around her desk to greet us. She was of medium stature, with gray hair pulled up on top of her head. She was dressed in a long skirt and a perfectly white and starched blouse, fastened under her chin with a broach that bore a cameo of two hands clasped together in prayer.

"Good morning, gentlemen," she said cheerily. "I am Alice Featherstone, and welcome to Mary and Martha. Please, be seated. Sylvia will take your coats and hats. Please, make yourselves comfortable."

"Thank you, madam," replied Holmes. "We thank you as well for agreeing to meet with us, although I fear that the reasons for our visit are not entirely the most pleasing to you, but we trust that our time together, to be held in strictest confidence, will be to the benefit of all concerned."

Miss Featherstone gave Holmes a bit of a queer look and then broke out into a pleasant and friendly laugh. "My goodness, Mr. Holmes, it sounded as if you have been rehearsing that little speech all the way from Windermere. Please, sir, we know exactly why you are here and I assure you that I and all of my staff will be as forthcoming as we possibly can, and I promise that we are as concerned as you to solve the matter that brought you. The tragic death of Cynthia Lazenby last year was devastating to all of us. We are entirely at your beck and call for the day."

"Ah, that is very gracious of you," said Holmes. "I feared that there might be some reticence on your part as the matters are somewhat delicate. Your unconditional assistance is most welcome."

"Oh my dear, Mr. Holmes, I never said that there were no conditions. There is, in fact, one very serious condition and it is insurmountable. You will have to agree to it or I will have no choice but to show you the door." There was a hint of laughter in her voice as she spoke and the genuine, perhaps even mischievous, smile never departed from her friendly face.

"Oh is there now?" queried Holmes. "And just what might that condition be?"

"Sir, we do everything we can to make life pleasant here at Mary and Martha for our guests, the young ladies entrusted to our care. They have been through quite a lot, what with their having been taken advantage of by older men, the judgment of their families and neighbors, and the physical trauma of pregnancy. So we offer as enjoyable and supportive time here as we can, but frankly, it does get rather boring and opportunities for anything unusual and diverting are rare. So here is our condition. You must give a talk to all of our guests. I have read of your famous lecture, *The Science of Deduction,* and some form of it would be very well received. And you Dr. Watson, you must tell them one of the fascinating stories of a mystery solved by Sherlock Holmes. That, gentlemen, is our only condition, but we will not back down on demanding it."

Holmes and I both laughed. "I believe," said Holmes, "that although very demanding we can meet your condition. However, forgive my asking, but will your young ladies find the details of some of the nefarious crimes I recount to be disturbing to their constitutions?"

This comment brought another spontaneous laugh from Miss Featherstone. "Oh, my dear Mr. Holmes, the guests in our care range in age from fourteen to forty and I hate to be the one to disillusion you, but firstly, by the time a young lady arrives here in her fifth or later month she has already gone through no end of issues with her defecation, urination, lactation and bleeding and is far beyond any queasiness associated with bodily functions. And secondly, it should be patently obvious by their condition that their discovery of the facts of life is already in the past. They are not cloistered little angels, sir. I do not believe that you will be able to shock or even disturb them. So go ahead and be as explicit as you wish. They will love having their spines tingled and their blood warmed."

"Very well then, we shall treat them as full-fledged adults. When is the lecture and story to take place?"

"They are gathered in the hall now waiting for you. When I announced at breakfast that we were to be visited by Sherlock Holmes and Dr. Watson they became positively giddy with excitement. Our home here may be founded on conservative evangelical principles, but that does not restrict multiple copies of *The Strand* from appearing here every month and being joyfully consumed by candlelight well after lights out. You will be addressing your fervent fans, gentlemen."

She rose and we followed her to the assembly hall. A group of about sixty young women stood and applauded as we entered. After being enthusiastically introduced by the Director, Holmes took his place behind the lecture and delivered his polished and familiar lecture. When he gave the explicit details of some murderous crime several shouts of fear were heard but not one of the audience members took the time to faint as that would have caused them to miss the next licentious detail in the story. He did, however, refrain from any mention of vampires.

When it came to my turn, I recited one of my favorite stories, *The Adventure of the Yellow-Face*. It was one in which no real crime was committed, although suspected, and it ended tenderly with a loving embrace between a man, his wife and her child by another man. I could see some tears upon some of the faces. When the assembly was over, both Holmes and I stood at the back of the hall, like local vicars after mass, and shook the hands of everyone of our listeners. Many of them let us know how much they enjoyed our being with them and announced which of the stories in *The Strand* had been their favorite.

Upon return to the Director's office the happy exchanges of the previous hour ended and we got down to matters much more serious.

Miss Featherstone began with a perfunctory account of the Mary and Martha Home. Back in 1875, a group of religious enthusiasts had started meeting down the road in the town of Keswick, on Derwentwater. Their initial meeting had grown into a very large gathering of several thousand believers who met for a week every summer for prayer and biblical teaching. After one such meeting, now ten years ago, a group of the wives were moved to do something more than just sit and listen. They decided that since they could not serve as missionaries on some foreign strand, they would begin their mission work right here in England. They identified the group they wished to minister to as those who were considered by society to be "fallen women" and who, in the minds of these good Christian women were "more sinned against than sinning" and in need of Christian compassion. They took as their guiding light the words of the Lord — "Neither do I condemn thee; go and sin no more." Their diligent research revealed to them, to their dismay, that most of the young "unwed mothers" had been victims of their employers, the sons of wealthy local merchants or minor nobility and, most distressingly, older family members and neighbors.

It took several years of "waiting on the Lord for the funds needed" — a process that might have included the twisting of the arms of various members of their families and friends — but finally several thousand pounds had been received and the home constructed. They were convinced that the model of the Lord Himself, who taught us all to love rather than judge, was the path they would follow and the young women they took under their care would be won over to a life of faith and purity by genuine Christian love.

Everything had been going quite swimmingly until that tragic night a year ago when Miss Cynthia Lazenby, a particularly independent-minded young woman, was out on the property, having insisted on a walk in the moonlight. She took such walks often and it was suspected that she had a secret habit of smoking cigarettes, an activity that was expressly forbidden by the rules of the Home.

Miss Lazenby was a tall, buxom, red-headed lass from the Borders and had from time to time regaled some of the other guests with stories of her beating the daylights out of some unsuspecting local cad who had thought she might be easy prey. She was only clad in her nightdress and a long cloak over top, and she would laugh that the only creatures who would consider her immodest would be the owls. She took a heavy walking stick with her whenever she went out at night and even though it was past curfew, no one was overly concerned for her although they might have had a bit of pity for anyone she could chance to run into.

It was a year ago, on the night of September 25th, which was a Saturday night, Miss Featherstone informed us, that Cynthia had announced to the other girls in her cottage that she was "going for a prayer meeting with Saint Phillip of Morrisville." She often went out for either that meeting or with "His Lordship, the Duke of Virginia" and no one thought anything of it, except those who were concerned that tobacco might harm the health of her baby.

The clock in the front hall had just struck eleven when the girls in several of the cottages heard an inhuman scream. It was unlike anything they had heard in their lives and many of them screamed in fear in response. Several of the bolder ones rushed to the doors to look out. They saw Cynthia running towards the manor house, clutching her neck as she ran. She hammered on the door of the infirmary and the nurse appeared in a moment and took her inside. According to the nurse, Cynthia gasped, "It was a bat. That bloody vampire bat bit me." The nurse observed two distinct wounds on her neck, both being two small punctures about a half an inch apart. The nurse attempted to calm the girl and told her that it was nothing more than a nip and that a big, strong girl like Cynthia should not worry. It would all be better by the morning. Cynthia shouted at the nurse — her using curse words probably did not endear her to the lady — and said that she couldn't breathe and that her heart was "going all crazy." The nurse went and fetched a glass of water and when she returned Cynthia was unconscious and lying on the floor. At that point, the nurse sounded the alarm and one of the watchmen came and knocked on Miss Featherstone's door. She dressed and ran over to the infirmary but by the time she arrived the nurse was desperately slapping Cynthia, trying to revive her. At least a dozen of the other young ladies had run into the infirmary and were standing around shouting and all saying to do this or do that.

Cynthia's pulse had faded and within another five minutes, it had stopped. The nurse looked up at Miss Featherstone, absolutely terrified and said, "She's dead. She's dead." Some of the young ladies who were standing around began to cry and shout and collapse. It was a positively dreadful night. The girls were ordered back to their cottages, but some outright refused to leave. A doctor was sent for from the village, but it took over an hour for him to arrive and by that time poor Cynthia had begun to turn blue. He did nothing but pronounce her dead.

Her parents demanded an inquiry, which was held, and the other young ladies, the nurse, the watchman, and the Director were all closely questioned. The doctor suggested a verdict of heart failure brought on by sudden fright, but the judge was not convinced. He knew enough that healthy young mothers-to-be do not have their hearts stop and then take another fifteen minutes to die. He ruled that the death was "for causes unknown."

The young ladies who had been present and watched as Cynthia died were severely distraught. The story that she had been attacked by a vampire spread like wildfire among them and soon all of the guests at Mary and Martha were firmly convinced that a vampire, or perhaps more than one, was on the loose in the Lake District. To make matters worse, a story was heard of a very similar death that took place at another home for un-wed mothers in the same district. The St. Catherine of Siena Home in Buttermere was said to have also been visited by a vampire bat, but the Catholic Church used its influence to keep an inquiry from taking place and the event was, according to Miss Featherstone "hushed up."

"Are you aware," asked Holmes, "of yet more deaths of young women in this manner?"

The Director nodded quietly. "There are some forty homes across Great Britain whose progressive philosophy is quite similar in many ways to ours and while we are not formally affiliated with each other, we maintain a constant correspondence among ourselves and meet together once every two years for the mutual benefit of our guests, our staff, and our institutions. We met last in London in January of this current year. I was made aware of six other deaths that had taken place within our circle since the previous get-together. Two more were here in the Lake District, two over in Snowdonia, and two up in the Highlands."

"And did all of these involve an attack by a so-called vampire," asked Holmes.

"They did. We really did not know what course of action to take. All deaths were investigated by the local police and the medical officers and a variety of judgments had been reached. As several jurisdictions had been involved, there was no hope of organizing them."

"So what did you do?"

"You must understand, sir, that not only were we deeply concerned about the safety of our guests, but, quite frankly, rumors had begun to grow and we were afraid that if we did not move to soothe the minds of our young ladies and their parents we would soon all be out of business. So we agreed among ourselves on two courses of action. First, that all of us hire more night watchmen and have our grounds patrolled around the clock."

"And the second?"

The Director hesitated briefly before answering. "Please understand, sir, that when you are faced with a threat to your institution that is based on irrational but unshakable superstition, you have no choice but to fight fire with fire."

"I am afraid I do not follow you there, Madam."

"We let it be known that we were diligently following the traditional means of warding off vampires. Bulbs of garlic were placed above the doors and window frames. The young ladies were given a daily dose of a secret folk medicine, and all were given crosses to wear around their necks.

"Madam," said Holmes. "You are a devout Christian, and both you and your nurse have training in modern scientific medicine. Surely you are not telling me that you resorted to magic charms and potions to protect your clients against the specter of non-existent vampire bats?"

"It is embarrassing to admit, Mr. Holmes but that is exactly what we did. And as I sit here before you all I can say is that not only have the attacks ceased at all of the homes but our babies are healthier than ever and our young mothers are restored to full strength more rapidly than at any time in the past."

Holmes said nothing and briefly closed his eyes. I was expecting that he would give the good Miss Featherstone a severe tongue-lashing, and I was quite ready to second his opinion. Instead, he opened his eyes and quietly asked, "This daily medication you give to your guests: is it by chance supplied to you by the firm *Medical Miracles of Mole Valley*?"

"Why yes, Mr. Holmes, it is. I gather that you are familiar with this firm and its products. All of our guests and their families now swear by them. Not a day goes by that the young ladies do not take their daily capsule."

"Might you have a bottle of those capsules that I could look at briefly?"

"A bottle? I have a dozen cases of them. If you will excuse me a moment, I will bring a sample to you."

She rose and left the office, returning in a minute carrying in her hand a large bottle made of dark brown glass, and bearing white labels with printing on both the front and back. She placed it on the desk in front of us. The printing, in large blue letters read:

The Secret Carpathian Cure: Daily Medications for Expectant Mothers

Guaranteed to improve the health of mother and child, bring ease in delivery, and give protection against attacks of pernicious spirits, vampires, and all other evils to which mothers-to-be are subject.

Beneath the title were the directions for use, and they stated that two of the capsules were to be taken daily, at breakfast and supper times.

At the bottom of the label, in small but bold letters, I read:

Guaranteed effective or payment refunded. Store in a cool dark place.

Price:£3. Contents: 120 capsules.

I did some rapid calculation in my head. Every one of the young ladies was paying a shilling a day for what was no more than snake oil. Now it was my turn to challenge the wisdom, indeed the sanity of the Director. "Madam," I said sternly and with no small helping of anger. "I am shocked, shocked by what you have told us. Ancient potions from the Carpathians have absolutely no medicinal value and it is nothing more than a figment of disturbed imaginations to believe that vampires exist or that they can be warded off by taking magic pills. This nonsensical cure is nothing more than a monstrous fraud designed to separate gullible dupes from their income. That you would use the donations of your supporters to underwrite such a deceitful crime is beyond belief."

I had expected a strong response from her. What I received instead was an affirmative nod and a curious smile. "You are entirely correct, doctor. But before you completely condemn us let me tell you a few things that may alter your judgment. Firstly, not one cent of our supporters' funds is used for these purchases. We just add it to the monthly bills we send to the families, and none have objected to paying. And again, before passing judgment, please read the conditions on the back side of the bottle." She reached forward and turned the bottle around so that the print on the reverse side could be seen. I gave her a very skeptical look, but Holmes and I leaned forward so that we could read what was printed. It ran:

Guarantee subject to the following conditions:

1. **Capsules must be taken twice daily, without fail.**
2. **Mothers must refrain from the use of all forms of alcohol, tobacco, and coffee.**
3. **Mothers must drink a minimum of forty ounces of pure water per day and consume a minimum of three portions of fresh fruit and vegetables.**
4. **Red meats, sweets, and fried foods must be limited to one portion per week.**

5. **All mothers must engage in a minimum of thirty minutes of vigorous exercise daily, either in a gymnasium or outdoors.**

6. **Mothers must be seen by a registered nurse at least once a month and tested for any untoward medical conditions.**

As soon as we had finished reading these conditions the lady took the bottle away from us, opened it and shook out two capsules onto the desk.

"I invite you to try one, gentlemen. And please give them a good sharp bite."

Holmes and I both did as we were asked. The capsules were quite large, at least three-quarters of an inch in length. As I brought one of them to my mouth, I could smell the strong scent of garlic. I took it and clamped my teeth down on it.

The taste was exceptionally disagreeable. I could tell by the look on Holmes's face that he had the same reaction as I. The first sensation was of a sharp citrus flavor, some sort of concentrated lemon juice, and it was followed by a dreadful aftertaste of fish oil. Holmes and I looked at each other and both made faces such as a schoolboy might when forced to take his hated medicine.

Miss Featherstone broke out in a laugh and hastily opened the drawer of her desk and withdrew a small bowl of peppermints and placed it in front of us.

"Now, gentlemen, do you see why the Carpathian Cure has brought about healthier mothers and babies?"

"This is nothing more than a common antiscorbutic," I said, "mixed with cod liver oil, and placed inside a gelatin capsule that has been infused with garlic. It could be supplied for a penny a day, not a shilling."

"Of course, it could, Doctor Watson. But would anyone use it?"

"Most likely not," acknowledged Holmes. "Now permit me to ask, whence came this Carpathian Cure to your attention?"

"The owner of the Miracle Medicines of Mole Valley comes around every four months and takes an order and then it arrives within a fortnight by the post."

"And might that be a Dr. Romanescu?" queried Holmes.

"Yes, it is. You have indeed done your homework, young man."

"Does he provide you with a pamphlet, or any documentation attesting to the efficacy of the medicine?"

"He did several years ago when he was first trying to have us buy his product. He had some sort of translated article from a medical journal in Europe. But since the rumors of vampires started flying all he does now is renew his order sheet and then he runs back to the streams and lake to go fishing. It is odd to have a doctor arrive with his large bamboo case for his fishing rod strung over his back, but he is a shy chap and we assume that he prefers the lonely life of the complete angler to the noise of society."

"Does he provide similar services to the other affiliated homes?"

"I think there are nearly thirty of us now giving the girls their capsules every day. Dr. Grigore is completing a study comparing the health of the young ladies who take the capsules to those who do not. When it is published, I am quite certain that the rest of the homes will come on board."

"Please madam," I said, having held my tongue for as long as I could. "You cannot possibly believe that garlic flavored capsules containing common household medications are responsible for the improved health of your young mothers."

"My good doctor," she replied. "Of course not. The results are entirely achieved by adhering to the conditions on the back of the bottle, but without the cost and the threat of losing the guarantee, who would follow them? It is quite brilliant, is it not? And where is the harm?"

"I will warrant," I said, "that the irrational fear of vampires provides a far stronger motive than worrying about losing a guarantee."

"I have no doubt you are correct," she said. "But measure that against the improvement in the health of both mother and baby and again, what is the harm?"

I bristled in anger, but Holmes reached his hand over and calmly placed it on my arm. In a quiet voice, he asked, "I assume that you keep a log of your visitors. Would you be so kind as to check it for us and tell me if, by chance, this Dr. Romanescu visited Mary and Martha on September 24 of last year?"

The Director said nothing in reply. The smile had vanished from her face along with the color. Her eyes had widened and her hands had stopped any movement.

"That was not a question that you asked me, Mr. Holmes. It was an accusation, was it not?"

"It matters not the form. Would you mind terribly checking your log?"

"It is not necessary. I do recall quite clearly that Dr. Romanescu had been here the day before Cynthia's death." Here she paused and for several moments, neither she nor Holmes spoke. Then she continued. "Mr. Holmes, I hope you know what you are doing. You are bordering on slandering a man that we trust. If what you are alluding to is false then you are doing despicable damage to the reputation of a good man. If the aspersions you are casting are true, then we have made an error in judgment with horrible consequences."

Again she paused. "I believe gentlemen, that it would be appropriate for you to conclude your visit now and leave the Home. Your presentation to our guests was appreciated. I assume that the hotel's driver has waited for you."

She called for her secretary to fetch our coats and closed the door to her office as we departed.

Chapter Eight
Miss Holmes and the Vampire

I could see by the intense look that had entered Holmes's eyes that he was closing in on his prey and I ventured to ask "You have as much as accused the doctor of murder. Do you have any proof?"

"None. I shall have to find a way to capture him in his heinous act."

"How?"

"I do not know."

"He could strike again at any time, could he not?"

"Not until the Saturday closest to the full moon. At that time, I expect this dark and sinister specter to reappear."

With one exception the next three weeks were pleasant and uneventful. A nicely engraved invitation from Mr. and Mrs. William Armitage of Reading had arrived, inviting me to the private wedding of their son and Miss Helen Stoner, to be held on the sixth of

October. I sent a note back promising to attend although I thought it might be wise to bring my doctor's bag along with me in the likely chance that the mother might not make it through the ceremony without going into labor.

I had set up a small office near Marylebone Station and the occasional appearance of a patient had increased to a modest trickle. So every morning I was out of Baker Street by eight o'clock. Yet every morning when I sat down for breakfast, Sherlock Holmes was already up and gone. He returned late in the evenings and beyond a friendly greeting and some idle chit-chat we talked little and he said nothing about Miss Stoner, or the doctor from Transylvania, or the spectred bats. I was burning with curiosity but had already learned that it was useless to query him on matters that he was not ready to reveal. In his own good time, he would tell me his stories.

The exception to the routine was a note I found sitting beside my breakfast place one morning. It was from Holmes and read:

Strike the Roma off the list. On August 5, having heard that a young woman was attacked by a vampire bat, and being the sensible folk that they are and wanting none of that, they up and left Stoke Moran and have not been seen in the area since.

A second note appeared on the morning of Thursday, September 30. It was also sitting by my breakfast place and read:

If convenient, please cancel your appointments for Saturday afternoon and come back here by five o'clock. There is a distinct element of danger. S.H.

I confess that my patients that day did not have my undivided attention. I kept glancing up at the clock to see if four-thirty had arrived. As soon as it had I was on my way to Baker Street. When I entered our front room, I was greeted not only by Holmes but by the lovely and radiant Miss Helen Stoner, who now resembled a balloon about to explode. Beside her sat Inspector Lestrade.

"Welcome Watson. The game is afoot. We really must have a doctor on hand just in case young master or miss Armitage decides to arrive early."

"Good heavens, Holmes. You cannot possibly be planning to involve Miss Stoner in any sort of outing. As a doctor, I simply will not stand for it."

"No, no," said Holmes. "We only need her to help create the appearance of an outing, is that not right, Inspector."

"It is completely cocked-up if you ask me," Lestrade said. "But if it works and we catch a murderer in the act then it will be worth a try."

"What in the world," I demanded, "is going on?"

"Miss Stoner," said Holmes, "sent a note two weeks ago to Stoke Moran letting them know that she would be returning there this Saturday evening on the pretense that she could fetch all of her belongings and then the next day return to Reading to prepare for her wedding. I am predicting that a vampire will be waiting for her and we shall have a stake ready to drive through his evil heart."

"You are not about to use her as bait in your trap, Holmes. I will not permit it."

"I promise you, my dear friend, that she will be securely and comfortably situated and not in the least bit of danger. But we must have her make the necessary appearances else the plan will never work. Now come. The three men will exit the back door as the lady leaves by the front. We will take separate cabs to Waterloo and meet up in our cabin on the train.

Miss Stoner looked up at me. The lovely face that had been distorted by fear just four weeks ago was now radiant. Her complexion was cherubic and her smile and eyes dancing with happiness. "It is quite alright, Dr. Watson. I thank you again just as I did when I sat here four weeks ago for your concern for me. But other than feeling more awkward than a one-ton turtle I am doing well, and I admit that if I can play my part in solving the mystery of the death of my sister I will be a very happy mother indeed. I shall see you on the train."

With the ever-faithful Mrs. Hudson helping her, she slowly descended the seventeen steps from our rooms to the pavement of Baker Street. As instructed by Holmes, the three men exited into the back alley and caught a cab on Marylebone Road.

By six o'clock we had arrived at Waterloo. The temperature had dropped and the sun had set. The sky was clear and I expected that a full harvest moon would soon be rising from the eastern horizon. We watched from a distance as Miss Stoner quite visibly made her way through the front door of the station. It was impossible for anyone not to notice her and several women stopped to ask if she needed help getting to the train.

Lestrade led us through a back entrance, used by the station master and, when necessary, Scotland Yard. Unseen, we boarded the train from the engineer's door and walked back in the corridor half the length of it until we came to our cabin. Miss Stoner was already sitting and waiting for us. Five minutes after the train pulled out Holmes excused himself and left the cabin. Fifteen minutes later the door of the cabin opened. For a second the three of us looked up in shocked silence and then we all dissolved into unstoppable gales of laughter. For there in front of us, covered in a long hooded cape and bearing lovely locks of dark hair was an enormously pregnant Sherlock Holmes. Lestrade was beside himself, convulsed with laughs. I was quite sure that it would be the only time in my life that I would see tears rolling down his cheeks. I was fearful that Miss Stoner might give birth on the spot, brought on by the shaking and convulsing of her body. She bit against the fleshy part of her hand in an effort to stop. As soon as she removed it from her mouth she began to laugh again.

At first, Holmes just glared at the three of us, but uncontrolled laughter is one of the most contagious of human conditions and soon he was chuckling along with us.

"Good Lord, Holmes," said Lestrade. "It will be the vampire who will die of fright." He could say no more as he broke out laughing again.

"Laugh all you want," said Holmes. "From a distance, and in the dark, I shall make a perfectly good substitute for a mother-to-be."

"Where is our Yard photographer when I need him?" sputtered Lestrade. "No one will ever believe me when I tell them who I shared a train cabin with. Miss Shirley Holmes, the ugliest mother in all of England." He laughed some more."

Once we had wiped away our tears, Lestrade gained control of himself and spoke. "So then, Miss Holmes, let me get this straight. The real mother-to-be is to exit the train and meet you in the station lavatory." He had to stop again as he said, "And what if seven old ladies are stuck in the lavatory when Miss Holmes enters. We will have to call the riot squad."

He bit into his lower lip and then continued. "Then you are to walk from the station to Stoke Moran and you believe that while doing so you will be attacked by a vampire and then Watson and I will run out and hold him down so you can drive a stake through his heart." He laughed again. "Watson, I hope you have a stake in you medical bag. Will a scalpel do the trick?"

We settled down for the remainder of the short journey. By the time we arrived at the Leatherhead Station twilight had vanished, but the platform and streets were visible in the light of the gas lamps and the glow from the full moon. The three men exited first from the far side of the train and hustled our way unseen around the front of the engine and into the station by a service door. Miss Stoner waited until the car had emptied and then she slowly descended the steps to the platform. Again two women took pity on her and helped her onto the platform. She made her way directly to the station lavatory, as would be expected of a woman in her advanced state. We waited a full ten minutes until all of the other passengers had departed and then she reappeared, except it was not her but rather Miss Shirley Holmes and I had to admit he, or she, was entirely convincing. The hood was pulled around his head, almost concealing his gaunt face and hawk-like nose. The cloak was, from a distance, indistinguishable from that worn by Miss Stoner. He was waddling slowly and holding on to handrails as he struggled down the stairs, fearful of toppling over onto a massive distended tummy.

A few minutes later the lights of the station were turned off and Lestrade made his way to the door of the ladies' lavatory. He knocked on it gently and Miss Stoner appeared. He led her into the station master's office where a constable was quietly waiting for her. Then he and I hurried to catch up with a slowly moving Holmes.

On all other occasions when I have walked with Sherlock Holmes he strode purposefully and quickly. This time, he was slow and deliberate and utterly convincing. Lestrade and I stayed well back of him, in total silence, a chill wind blowing in our face. In the moonlight, he looked like a shadowy specter plodding his way out of the town and up the road to Stoke Moran. Far away we could hear the deep tones of the parish clock striking the ninth hour. It was a full three-quarters of an hour before Holmes reached the entrance to the laneway of the estate and it was there that we could see him stop. In the moonlit sky, I saw a speck, a dark object dancing and darting like a bat. As it came flying toward him, he deftly ducked and evaded being struck. The bat returned a few seconds later and came darting for his neck. Holmes, a trained pugilist, swerved to one side just as he would to evade a left hook. Again the bat missed him. A third time the bat descended on him, this time aiming directly for his chest. It struck him. As it did, he swiftly brought his hand down on it and in the same motion placed it on the ground and under his foot. He then began to move hand over hand, furiously, as if pulling on an invisible string.

"Watson! Lestrade! You see him? He is in the clearing behind the fence. After him!"

With a bum leg left over from my service in Afghanistan, I am no runner. But Lestrade was running flat out up the dark road. He hurdled the fence and ran into the clearing that we thought Holmes had directed us to. There he stopped and looked around. "Which way, which way Holmes?" he shouted.

I caught up but could see no one. As I approached him, my foot kicked what felt like a long stick. Suddenly it moved and I jumped back in panic. What, in the name of the devil, was it? It moved again and then started to slide across the grass directly towards the approaching Holmes, who was still pumping his hands as if gathering twine. The end of the long stick abruptly rose from the ground and landed in Holmes's hand.

"Gentlemen, meet the vampire."

In Holmes's hand was an exceptionally long fly-fishing rod. "Come quickly," he said. "He may have run to the house." Holmes held the rod in one hand and the three of us, including a still bulging Holmes, ran towards the Stoke Moran Manor House. In the moonlight, we approached a very old mansion with gray gables and a high roof-tree. It was in darkness, but we entered and found the hallway lamps and lit the way down the corridors. Holmes had doffed his tummy and we walked quickly from room to room, lighting lamps and searching. I had my service revolver in my hand, as did Lestrade.

We found nothing.

After a half hour, we gathered in the kitchen.

"Was whatever attacked you what I think it was?" asked Lestrade.

From the pocket of his cloak, he extracted a strange thing and carefully unfolded it. It was a silk-covered object that when stretched out resembled the shape of a small bat. "Herein the bat; the spectred bat. Be very careful of his teeth," said Holmes. He pointed to two pins that protruded from the front of the head. "They have been dipped in curare. If they were to pierce your skin, you would be dead within twenty minutes."

"If that vampire bat is a murder weapon," said Lestrade, "it has to be the most diabolically clever one I have ever seen."

"Yes," said Holmes. "The devil himself was behind it. Our Dr.

Romanescu appears to have constructed it and affixed it to the end of his fishing line and then expertly flung it, as he would a tied fly, at his victims. After years of pursuing his hobby of fly fishing, he had become deadly accurate at aiming and landing his flies exactly where he wanted."

"Holmes," I said. "I saw that thing strike you directly in the chest. But there has been no effect on you. What happened?"

Holmes undid the buttons on his shirt. "I knew that I had little chance of stopping the bat before it struck me, so I had a thick leather shirt and leggings made up that I knew a set of pins could not penetrate. They protected my body and neck otherwise, I would be just another dead mother-to-be. They made walking rather awkward, but that added to the desired effect."

"All well and good," said Lestrade. "However, we have a murderer on the loose and we need to find him before he strikes again. I'll have officers all over this place in the morning and we should be able to round up any of the local ruffians he used to assist him. But we still need to track him down."

Holmes nodded and the three of us got up from the kitchen chairs, extinguished the lights in the house, and walked back to the station. There we met Miss Stoner and she assured us that she had been quite comfortable. We caught the late train back to Waterloo. Lestrade had a police carriage bring us back to Baker Street where Mrs. Hudson took charge of our almost mother and I fell into my bed and slept. Holmes sat in his chair and lit his pipe.

On Monday morning, a motley crew assembled around our breakfast table. Mrs. Armitage, the protective mother-in-law-to-be, the prospective mother-to-be, Miss Stoner, Inspector Lestrade, Holmes and I all enjoyed a nourishing meal. Miss Stoner did not drink the coffee.

Lestrade said, "We have a bulletin out all over the country for your doctor. But no one has seen hide or hair of him. We expect that he will try to get across the channel and back to Romania. Quite the diabolically clever fellow."

"Our Doctor Grigore may have begun his terrible deeds over a decade ago in Romania," said Holmes.

"The death of Mr. Stoner, the diplomat?" I asked.

"Most likely. He saw an opportunity to leave a poor country and become wealthy and comfortable in England. The unfortunate widow, Mrs. Stoner, was his next victim. I have to assume that he was not aware of the terms of her will until after her death, and then he had to make sure that neither of the daughters married or reached the age of twenty-one. He would have been left with nothing."

"He had the income from the firm, did he not?" I said.

"The firm, as Miss Stoner and her sister discovered, had precious little income," said Holmes. "He had to find a way to increase it substantially and he came up with a scheme that combined his skill in fly fishing, his knowledge of and access to poisons, and the national mania about vampires. He merely disposed of enough young mothers-to-be to get a panic going and soon they were all buying his secret formula."

Lestrade asked, "All quite logical, just as you like it, Holmes. But how did you ever connect fly-fishing as the means of delivering the poison?"

"Why, Inspector, simply by following the methods and practices for which Scotland Yard is justly famous."

"You'll forgive me," said Lestrade, "if I do not waste a second of my time believing that one. Now cut out the clever jibes and just answer my question."

"A diligent detective," said Holmes, "is obligated to seek data that will confirm or deny everything he has been told. I was informed that the doctor was an expert in fishing and so I made a visit to the Royal Society for the Promotion and Protection of Piscatorial Pursuits and inquired if they had ever heard of Dr. Romanescu. They had not only heard of him but acknowledged that, on several occasions, he had won the prize at numerous field events and had twice taken the honors at the contests held indoors at the Wembley Armories. They set up archery targets both lying on the ground and propped up and the angler has to cast his fly, attached to a small pin, and land it in the bulls-eye. Our doctor was quite the expert in doing so. All he had to do was to design a small bat-like object and send it off while hidden from view, and prick his victims with a set of pins that he had dipped in curare.

"I also scrupulously confirmed that he had made visits to many homes for expectant mothers throughout Britain and had been present at the other locations on or around the dates that young women died there. The ensuing rumors and fears greatly increased his sales of his so-called secret formula and having had success in doing so he used the same method to murder his stepdaughter and protect his income."

He paused and slowly shook his head. "The manifold wickedness of the human heart is beyond imagination. When a clever man turns his brain to crime, it is the worst of all. And when a doctor goes wrong, he is the first of criminals. He has the nerve and the knowledge."

Epilogue

Anotice was issued to the press and posted in every train station and post office in the country. A picture of Dr. Romanescu was attached and many sightings of him were reported. Sadly all proved false. He had flown the coup and was widely believed to have escaped the Continent.

There was, however, some joyful news. Holmes and I accepted the invitations to Reading and were present at the small wedding of Mr. and Mrs. Percy Armitage. I do not believe I have ever seen a more radiant and more beautiful bride, nor one more likely to burst her water while standing at the altar. A healthy baby boy was born two weeks later and I was honored to be the doctor chosen by Helen to assist in the delivery. It is my hope that his education will be *sans* vampires.

Three weeks later the unit of the Coldstream Guards was sent on an exchange exercise to Austria. The young Lieutenants Percy Armitage and Peter Bennion-Bowen went with their regiment, leaving Mrs. Helen Armitage in genteel comfort in Reading with her mother-in-law, who was wonderfully enraptured with her first grandchild. Mrs. Bennion-Bowen was deeply worried about the spirits of her son Peter as he was still grieving for the loss of his beloved Julia. She followed him to the Continent in order to provide the encouragement that only mothers can give to their sons and found temporary lodgings in Vienna.

Two months after the fateful night on the laneway of Stoke Moran the Foreign Office reported that the nefarious Dr. Grigore Romanescu had been seen in Bucharest. Our diplomats at the Embassy there immediately placed demands for his return to England to face trial and most likely the gallows. Such agreements between countries that are not particularly friendly with each other do not happen quickly and Mycroft advised us that it could take many months to bring the murderer back, if it ever happened at all.

I returned to my practice and Holmes to his role as the country's only consulting detective and both of us continued to enjoy our accommodations in Baker Street, where Mrs. Hudson tolerated our sometimes strange behavior and made sure that we were properly fed, including at least three daily servings of fresh fruit and vegetables.

And so it was at supper time one day in March of 1888 that our bell sounded on Baker Street. Mrs. Hudson opened it and immediately confident footsteps were heard ascending our stairs. Inspector Lestrade walked in unannounced and pulled up a chair at the table.

"Some news just came in on the wire that I thought you might want to hear."

"Well now," said Holmes. "It must be a bit of a stunner to bring you over here while your good wife is waiting for you with your dinner ready."

"A stunner it is. The Kingdom of Romania has agreed to the extradition of Dr. Romanescu. We had a team of officers ready to head off there on Monday and bring him back to London."

Holmes gave him a bit of a look. "What do you mean, we *had?*"

"Called it off… there is no point bringing back a dead man."

"Indeed?" said Holmes. "Poisoned?"

"Or bitten by a vampire?" I offered.

Lestrade shook his head. "Both wrong. Somebody cut his throat."

Did you enjoy this story? Are there ways it could have been improved? Please help the author and future readers of future New Sherlock Holmes Mysteries by posting a review on the site from which you purchased this book. Thanks, and happy sleuthing and deducing.

Historical Notes

Victorian England was fascinated and titillated by stories of vampires. In 1871, Sheridan Le Fanu wrote *Carmilla*, the story of a young woman named Laura, who was all too susceptible to the seductive entrapments of a beautiful female vampire. With its thinly disguised hints of a lesbian attraction between the two young females the story proved to be irresistible to the famously repressed Victorians. In 1897, Bram Stoker wrote and published the renowned novel *Dracula*. It sold in the millions and has never since been out of print. When not penning provocative novels, Mr. Abraham Stoker served as the capable manager of the Lyceum Theatre and the professional agent of Henry Irving, the most successful actor in the West End during the days of Sherlock Holmes and Dr. Watson.

The Roma people, incorrectly referred to as Gypsies, were the targets of many false prejudices during the time of Sherlock Holmes. They still are today.

In 1875, a religious movement began in Keswick in the Lake District that evolved into the influential annual Keswick Conventions. These gatherings, which continue into the present day, inspired all sorts of humanitarian, missionary and spiritual enterprises.

The Lake Poets — William Wordsworth, Samuel Taylor Coleridge, and Robert Southey — wrote some of the most admired and influential poetry of the Romantic era while living in the various villages of the Lake District, the loveliest part of England's green and pleasant land.

About the Author

In May of 2014 the Sherlock Holmes Society of Canada – better known as The Bootmakers (www.torontobootmakers.com) – announced a contest for a new Sherlock Holmes story. Although he had no experience writing fiction, the author submitted a short Sherlock Holmes mystery and was blessed to be declared one of the winners. Thus inspired, he has continued to write new Sherlock Holmes Mysteries since. He is on a mission now to write sixty new Sherlock Holmes mysteries — one inspired by each story in the original canon.

In real life he writes about and serves as a consultant for political campaigns in Canada and the USA (www.ConservativeGrowth.net), but would abandon that pursuit if he could possibly earn a decent living writing about Sherlock Holmes. He currently writes from Toronto, Tokyo, and Manhattan.

New Sherlock Holmes Mysteries
by Craig Stephen Copland

www.SherlockHolmesMystery.com

Available from Amazon as either ebook or paperback.

The Adventure of the Beryl Anarchists. A deeply distressed banker enters 221B Baker St. His safe has been robbed and he is certain that his motorcycle-riding sons have betrayed him. Highly incriminating and embarrassing records of the financial and personal affairs of England's nobility are now in the hands of blackmailers - the Beryl Anarchists - all passionately involved in the craze of motorcycle riding, and in ruthless criminal pursuits.

And then a young girl is murdered. Holmes and Watson must find the real culprits and stop them before more crimes are committed - too horrendous to be imagined.

This new mystery was inspired by *The Adventure of the Beryl Coronet* and borrows the setting and some of the characters. And, of course, our beloved Sherlock Holmes and Dr. Watson are there, just as they are in the original Canon.

The Adventure of the Coiffered Bitches. A
beautiful young woman will soon inherit an lot of money. She
disappears. Her little brother is convinced that she has become a
zombie, living and not living in the graveyard of the ruined old
church.

Another young woman - flirtatious, independent, lovely - agrees
to be the nurse to the little brother. She finds out far too much and,
in desperation seeks help from Sherlock Holmes, the man she also
adores.

Sherlock Holmes, Dr. Watson and Miss Violet Hunter must
solve the mystery of the coiffered bitches, avoid the massive mastiff
that could tear their throats, and protect the boy.

The story is inspired by the original Conan Doyle "Adventure of
the Copper Beeches." Fans of the original Sherlock Holmes will
enjoy seeing the same characters in a brand new murder mystery.

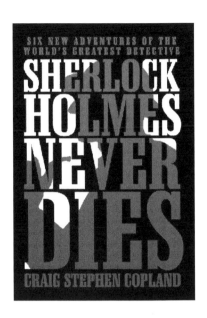

SIX NEW ADVENTURES OF THE WORLD'S GREATEST DETECTIVE
SHERLOCK HOLMES NEVER DIES
CRAIG STEPHEN COPLAND

Sherlock Holmes Never Dies. Return to Baker Street, where the world's most famous detective encounters six new cases that require his expert touch. London's super sleuth, Sherlock Holmes, sets out with long suffering Watson as the detectives of Scotland Yard are stumped yet again.

Blood coats the street of Victorian England, but no evidence is clear and no suspect cleared of guilt. As to be expected, evil genius— the Napoleon of Crime—Professor Moriarty soon reappears. The great detective must thwart his diabolical machinations, but even Holmes is practically brought to his knees by shocking new discoveries only he can understand.

Despite Moriarty's conniving, Sherlock will use the science of deduction to unravel mysteries of theft, abduction, political intrigue, and murder. Female characters take much deserved center stage in these updated stories, no longer willing to play the part of hapless victim or jealous wife. Meanwhile, Holmes and Watson traipse the globe in search of justice. No guilty party is safe, no matter the distance, from the all-knowing eye of the world's best detective and his devoted friend.

Studying Scarlet. Starlet O'Halloran (who bears a distinct resemblance to the South's most famous heroine) has arrived in London looking for her long lost husband Brett. She and Momma come to 221B Baker Street seeking the help of Sherlock Holmes. Three men have already been murdered, garroted, by an evil conspiracy.

Unexpected events unfold and together Sherlock Holmes, Dr. Watson, Starlet, Brett, and two new members of the clan have to vanquish a band of murderous anarchists, rescue the King and save the British Empire. This is an unauthorized parody inspired by Arthur Conan Doyle's *A Study in Scarlet* and Margaret Mitchell's *Gone with the Wind.*

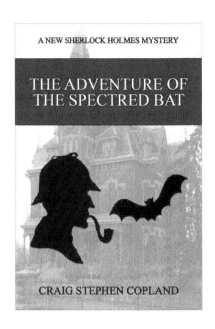

The Adventure of the Spectred Bat. A beautiful young woman, just weeks away from giving birth, arrives at Baker Street in the middle of the night. Her sister was attacked by a bat and died and now it is attacking her.

Could it be a vampire sent by the local band of Gypsies? Sherlock Holmes and Dr. Watson are called upon to investigate. The step-father, the local Gypsies and the furious future mother-in-law are all suspects. And was it really a vampire in the shape of a bat that took the young mother-to-be's life? This adventure takes the world's favorite detective away from London to Surrey north to the lovely but deadly Lake District.

If you enjoy both stories about Sherlock Holmes and about vampires, you will love this one.

The story was inspired by the original Sherlock Holmes story, "The Adventure of the Speckled Band" and like the original, leaves the mind wondering and the heart racing.

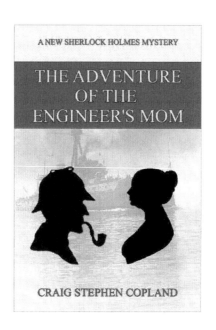

The Adventure of the Engineer's Mom. A brilliant young Cambridge University engineer is carrying out secret research for the Admiralty.

It will lead to the building of the world's most powerful battleship, The Dreadnaught.

His adventuress mother is kidnapped and having been spurned by Scotland Yard he seeks the help of Sherlock Holmes.

Was she taken by German spies, or an underhanded student, or by someone else? Whoever it was is prepared to commit cold-blooded murder to get what they want.

Holmes and Watson have help from an unexpected source – the engineer's mom herself.

This new mystery is inspired by the original Sherlock Holmes story – The Engineer's Thumb. It is set in the same era in England and you will encounter several of the original characters, but now in a completely new traditional Sherlock Holmes mystery.

100

The Bald-Headed Trust. Watson insists on taking Sherlock Holmes on a short vacation to the seaside in Plymouth. No sooner has Holmes arrived than he is needed to solve a double murder and prevent a massive fraud diabolically designed by the evil Professor himself.

Moriarty has found a way to deprive the financial world of millions of pounds without their ever knowing that they have been robbed.

Who knew that a family of devout conservative churchgoers could come to the aid of Sherlock Holmes and bring enormous grief to evil doers? The story is inspired by *The Red-Headed League*, one of the original stories in the canon of Sherlock Holmes by Sir Arthur Conan Doyle.

The Adventure of the Notable Bachelorette. A snobbish and obnoxious nobleman enters 221B Baker Street demanding the help of Sherlock Holmes in finding his much younger wife – a beautiful and spirited American from the West.

Three days later the wife is accused of a vile crime. Now she comes to Sherlock Holmes seeking his help to prove her innocence so she can avoid the gallows.

Neither noble husband nor wife have been playing by the rules of Victorian moral behavior.

So who did it? The wife? The mistress? The younger brother? Someone unknown?

Fan of Sherlock Holmes will enjoy this mystery, set in London during the last years of the nineteenth century, and written in the same voice as the beloved stories of the original canon. This new mystery was inspired by the original Sherlock Holmes story, *The Adventure of the Noble Bachelor*.

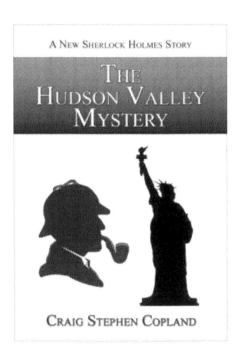

A NEW SHERLOCK HOLMES STORY

THE
HUDSON VALLEY
MYSTERY

CRAIG STEPHEN COPLAND

The Hudson Valley Mystery. A young man in New York went mad and murdered his father. Or so say the local police and doctors.

His mother knows he is innocent and knows he is not crazy. She appeals to Sherlock Holmes and together with Dr. and Mrs. Watson he crosses the Atlantic to help this client in need. Once there they must duel with the villains of Tammany Hall and with the specter of the legendary headless horseman.

This new Sherlock Holmes mystery was inspired by *The Buscombe Valley Mystery*.

A Case of Identity Theft. It is the fall of 1888 and Jack the Ripper is terrorizing London.

The national Rugby Union team has just returned from New Zealand and Australia. A young married couple are found, minus their heads. They were both on the team tour.

Another young couple is missing and in peril. Sherlock Holmes, Dr. Watson, the couple's mothers, and Mycroft must join forces to find the murderer before he kills again and makes off with half a million pounds. The novella is inspired by the original story by Arthur Conan Doyle, *A Case of Identity*. It will appeal both to devoted fans of Sherlock Holmes, as well as to those who love the great game of rugby.

The Sign of the Third. Fifteen hundred years ago the courageous Princess Hemamali smuggled the sacred tooth of the Buddha into Ceylon. Since that time it has never left the Temple of the Tooth in Kandy, where it has been guarded and worshiped by the faithful. Now, for the first time, it is being brought to London to be part of a magnificent exhibit at the British Museum.

But what if something were to happen to it? It would be a disaster for the British Empire. Sherlock Holmes, Dr. Watson and even Mycroft Holmes are called upon to prevent such a crisis. Will they prevail? What is about to happen to Dr. John Watson? And who is this mysterious young Irregular they call The Injin? This novella is inspired by the Sherlock Holmes mystery, *The Sign of the Four*. The same characters and villains are present, and fans of Arthur Conan Doyle's Sherlock Holmes will enjoy seeing their hero called upon yet again to use his powers of scientific deduction to thwart dangerous and dastardly criminals.

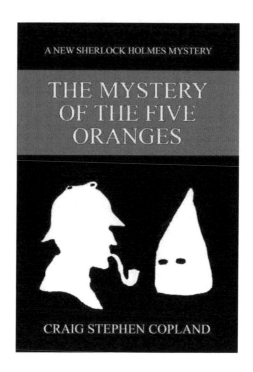

The Mystery of the Five Oranges. On a miserable rainy evening a desperate father enters 221B Baker Street. His daughter has been kidnapped and spirited off the North America. The evil network who have taken her have spies everywhere. If he goes to Scotland Yard they will kill her. There is only one hope – Sherlock Holmes.

Holmes and Watson sail to a small corner of Canada, Prince Edward Island, in search of the girl. They find themselves fighting one of the most powerful and malicious organizations on earth – the Ku Klux Klan. But they are aided in their quest by the newest member of the Baker Street Irregulars, a determined and imaginative young redhead, and by the resources of the Royal Canadian Mounted Police.

Sherlockians will enjoy this new adventure of the world's most famous detective, inspired by the original story of The Five Orange Pips. And those who love Anne of Green Gables will thrill to see her recruited by Holmes and Watson to help in the defeat of crime.

A NEW SHERLOCK HOLMES MYSTERY

THE ADVENTURE
OF THE BLUE
BELT BUCKLE

CRAIG STEPHEN COPLAND

The Adventure of the Blue Belt Buckle. A young street urchin, one of the Baker Street Irregulars, discovers a man's belt and buckle under a bush in Hyde Park. He brings it to Sherlock Holmes, hoping for a reward. The buckle is unique and stunning, gleaming turquoise stones set in exquisitely carved silver; a masterpiece from the native American west.

A body of an American Indian is found in a hotel room in Mayfair. Scotland Yard seeks the help of Sherlock Holmes in solving the murder. The victim is the brilliant artist that created and wore the buckle.

A secret key is found leading Sherlock Holmes to a replica set of the Crown Jewels. The real Jewels, supposedly secure inside the Tower of London are in danger of being stolen or destroyed. The Queen's Diamond Jubilee, to be held in just a few months, could be ruined.

Sherlock Holmes, Dr. Watson, Scotland yard, the Home Office and even Her Majesty all team up to prevent a crime of unspeakable dimensions.

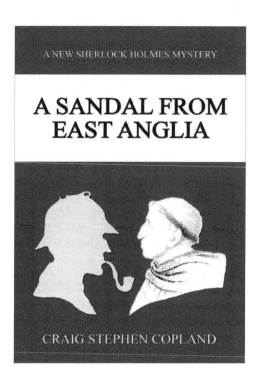

A SANDAL FROM EAST ANGLIA

CRAIG STEPHEN COPLAND

A Sandal from East Anglia. Archeological excavations at the ruined Abbey of St. Edmund unearth a sealed canister. In it is a document that has the potential to change the course of the British Empire and all of Christendom.

There are some evil young men who are prepared to rob, and beat and even commit murder to keep its contents from ever becoming known. There is a strikingly beautiful young Sister, with a curious double life, who is determined to use the document to improve the lives of women throughout the world.

Sherlock Holmes and Dr. Watson are called upon to protect the young woman, catch the killers, and trap the evil men who are greedily plotting against The Nun.

The mystery is inspired by the original Sherlock Holmes story, *A Scandal in Bohemia.* Fans of Sherlock Holmes will enjoy a new story that maintains all the loved and familiar characters and settings of Victorian England.

THE MAN WHO WAS TWISTED BUT HIP

CRAIG STEPHEN COPLAND

The Man Who Was Twisted But Hip. It is 1897 and France is torn apart by The Dreyfus Affair.

Westminster needs help from Sherlock Holmes to make sure that the evil tide of anti-Semitism that has engulfed France will not spread. A young officer in the Foreign Office suddenly resigns from his post and enters the theater. His wife calls for help from Sherlock Holmes.

The evil professor is up to something, and it could have terrible consequences for the young couple and all of Europe. Sherlock and Watson run all over London and Paris solving the puzzle and seeking to thwart Moriarty.

This new Sherlock Holmes mystery is inspired by the original story, *The Man with the Twisted Lip* as well as by the great classic by Victor Hugo, *The Hunchback of Notre Dame.*

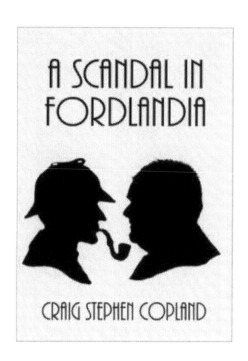

A SCANDAL IN FORDLANDIA

CRAIG STEPHEN COPLAND

A Scandal in Fordlandia. A satirical parody—this one inspired by *A Scandal in Bohemia* and set in Toronto in 2014.

Sherlock Holmes and Dr. Watson are visited by Toronto's famous mayor. He is desperate. When he was a teenager someone took some nasty photos of him. Those photos are now in the hands of his hated enemies, the Media. If they are made public, disaster could come not only upon those in the photo but on all of civilization as we know it. Holmes and Watson must retrieve the photos and save His Honour before chaos descends yet again on this most colorful politician.

Sherlock and Barack. This is NOT a new Sherlock Holmes Mystery. It is a Sherlockian research paper seeking answers to some very serious questions. Why did Barack Obama win in November 2012? Why did Mitt Romney lose? Pundits and political scientists have offered countless reasons.

This book reveals the truth - The Sherlock Holmes Factor. Had it not been for Sherlock Holmes, Mitt Romney would be president. This study is the first entry by Sherlockian Craig Stephen Copland into the Grand Game of amateur analysis of the canon of Sherlock Holmes stories, and their effect on western civilization.

Sherlockians will enjoy the logical deductions that lead to the inevitable conclusions.

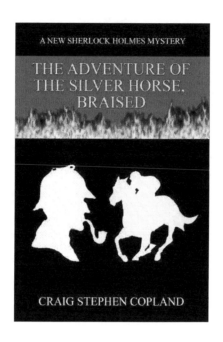

The Silver Horse, Braised. The greatest horse race of the century, with the best five-year-olds of England running against the best of America, will take place in a week at Epsom Downs. Millions have been bet on the winners. Owners, jockeys, grooms, and gamblers from across England arrive. So too do a host of colorful characters from the racetracks of America. Rumors of false statistics, threats, bribes, the administering of opiates to horse or rider, immoral seductions, abductions, and even murders are abounding. Scotland Yard is concerned. When a famous jockey is mysteriously killed while practicing on one of the favorites, Sherlock Holmes is called in.

Before the race, everything appears to be in order. The race is run and an incredible white horse emerges as the winner by over twenty-five lengths. Celebrations are in order and good times are had. And that night disaster strikes. More deaths, of both men and beasts, take place. Holmes identifies several suspects and then, to his great disappointment and frustration, he fails to prove that any of them committed the crime. Until . . . .

This completely original mystery is a tribute to the original

Sherlock Holmes story, Silver Blaze. It also borrows from the great racetrack stories of Damon Runyon. Fans of both of these wonderful writers will enjoy seeing Holmes, Watson, and Lestrade – assisted by Harry the Horse, Little Miss Marker, Sorrowful, and the nameless narrator – as they finally bring the culprits to justice.

Would you like to read another New Sherlock Holmes Mystery? They are all available immediately from Amazon.

You are invited to join the New Sherlock Holmes Mysteries mailing list and receive Irregular announcements about the release of new titles, special promotions and Sherlockian news. Go now to the website. www.SherlockHolmesMystery.com and sign up.

Privacy is promised.

Hey readers: The first day of every month is *New Sherlock Day*. All New Sherlock Holmes Mysteries ebooks on Kindle will go on sale for 99 cents for one day only. Watch for it at the start of each month.

The Adventure of the Speckled Band

The Original Sherlock Holmes Story

Arthur Conan Doyle

The Adventure of the Speckled Band

On glancing over my notes of the seventy odd cases in which I have during the last eight years studied the methods of my friend Sherlock Holmes, I find many tragic, some comic, a large number merely strange, but none commonplace; for, working as he did rather for the love of his art than for the acquirement of wealth, he refused to associate himself with any investigation which did not tend towards the unusual, and even the fantastic. Of all these varied cases, however, I cannot recall any which presented more singular features than that which was associated with the well-known Surrey family of the Roylotts of Stoke Moran. The events in question occurred in the early days of my association with Holmes, when we were sharing rooms as bachelors in Baker Street. It is possible that I might have placed them upon record before, but a promise of secrecy was made at the time, from which I have only been freed during the last month by the untimely death of the lady to whom the pledge was given. It is perhaps as well that the facts should now come to light, for I have reasons to know that there are widespread rumors as to the death of Dr. Grimesby Roylott which tend to make the matter even more terrible than the truth.

It was early in April in the year '83 that I woke one morning to find Sherlock Holmes standing, fully dressed, by the side of my bed. He was a late riser, as a rule, and as the clock on the mantelpiece showed me that it was only a quarter-past seven, I blinked up at him in some surprise, and perhaps just a little resentment, for I was myself regular in my habits.

"Very sorry to knock you up, Watson," said he, "but it's the common lot this morning. Mrs. Hudson has been knocked up, she retorted upon me, and I on you."

"What is it, then -- a fire?"

"No; a client. It seems that a young lady has arrived in a considerable state of excitement, who insists upon seeing me. She is waiting now in the sitting-room. Now, when young ladies wander about the metropolis at this hour of the morning, and knock sleepy people up out of their beds, I presume that it is something very pressing which they have to communicate. Should it prove to be an interesting case, you would, I am sure, wish to follow it from the outset. I thought, at any rate, that I should call you and give you the chance."

"My dear fellow, I would not miss it for anything."

I had no keener pleasure than in following Holmes in his professional investigations, and in admiring the rapid deductions, as swift as intuitions, and yet always founded on a logical basis with which he unraveled the problems which were submitted to him. I rapidly threw on my clothes and was ready in a few minutes to accompany my friend down to the sitting-room. A lady dressed in black and heavily veiled, who had been sitting in the window, rose as we entered.

"Good-morning, madam," said Holmes cheerily. "My name is Sherlock Holmes. This is my intimate friend and associate, Dr. Watson, before whom you can speak as freely as before myself. Ha! I am glad to see that Mrs. Hudson has had the good sense to light the fire. Pray draw up to it, and I shall order you a cup of hot coffee, for I observe that you are shivering."

"It is not cold which makes me shiver," said the woman in a low voice, changing her seat as requested.

"What, then?"

"It is fear, Mr. Holmes. It is terror." She raised her veil as she spoke, and we could see that she was indeed in a pitiable state of agitation, her face all drawn and gray, with restless frightened eyes, like those of some hunted animal. Her features and figure were those of a woman of thirty, but her hair was shot with premature gray, and her expression was weary and haggard. Sherlock Holmes ran her over with one of his quick, all-comprehensive glances.

"You must not fear," said he soothingly, bending forward and patting her forearm. "We shall soon set matters right, I have no doubt. You have come in by train this morning, I see."

"You know me, then?"

"No, but I observe the second half of a return ticket in the palm of your left glove. You must have started early, and yet you had a good drive in a dog-cart, along heavy roads, before you reached the station."

The lady gave a violent start and stared in bewilderment at my companion.

"There is no mystery, my dear madam," said he, smiling. "The left arm of your jacket is spattered with mud in no less than seven places. The marks are perfectly fresh. There is no vehicle save a dog-cart which throws up mud in that way, and then only when you sit on the left-hand side of the driver."

"Whatever your reasons may be, you are perfectly correct," said she. "I started from home before six, reached Leatherhead at twenty past, and came in by the first train to Waterloo. Sir, I can stand this strain no longer; I shall go mad if it continues. I have no one to turn to -- none, save only one, who cares for me, and he, poor fellow, can be of little aid. I have heard of you, Mr. Holmes; I have heard of you from Mrs. Farintosh, whom you helped in the hour of her sore need. It was from her that I had your address. Oh, sir, do you not think that you could help me, too, and at least throw a little light through the dense darkness which surrounds me? At present it is out of my power to reward you for your services, but in a month or six weeks I shall be married, with the control of my own income, and then at least you shall not find me ungrateful."

Holmes turned to his desk and, unlocking it, drew out a small case-book, which he consulted.

"Farintosh," said he. "Ah yes, I recall the case; it was concerned with an opal tiara. I think it was before your time, Watson. I can only say, madam, that I shall be happy to devote the same care to your case as I did to that of your friend. As to reward, my profession is its own reward; but you are at liberty to defray whatever expenses I may be put to, at the time which suits you best. And now I beg that you will lay before us everything that may help us in forming an opinion upon the matter."

"Alas!" replied our visitor, "the very horror of my situation lies in the fact that my fears are so vague, and my suspicions depend so entirely upon small points, which might seem trivial to another, that even he to whom of all others I have a right to look for help and advice looks upon all that I tell him about it as the fancies of a nervous woman. He does not say so, but I can read it from his soothing answers and averted eyes. But I have heard, Mr. Holmes, that you can see deeply into the manifold wickedness of the human heart. You may advise me how to walk amid the dangers which encompass me."

"I am all attention, madam."

"My name is Helen Stoner, and I am living with my stepfather, who is the last survivor of one of the oldest Saxon families in England, the Roylotts of Stoke Moran, on the western border of Surrey."

Holmes nodded his head. "The name is familiar to me," said he.

"The family was at one time among the richest in England, and the estates extended over the borders into Berkshire in the north, and Hampshire in the west. In the last century, however, four successive heirs were of a dissolute and wasteful disposition, and the family ruin was eventually completed by a gambler in the days of the Regency. Nothing was left save a few acres of ground, and the two-hundred-year-old house, which is itself crushed under a heavy mortgage. The last squire dragged out his existence there, living the horrible life of an aristocratic pauper; but his only son, my stepfather, seeing that he must adapt himself to the new conditions, obtained an advance from a relative, which enabled him to take a medical degree and went out to Calcutta, where, by his professional skill and his force of character, he established a large practice. In a fit of anger, however, caused by some robberies which had been perpetrated in the house, he beat his native butler to death and narrowly escaped a capital sentence. As it was, he suffered a long term of imprisonment and afterwards returned to England a morose and disappointed man.

"When Dr. Roylott was in India he married my mother, Mrs. Stoner, the young widow of Major-General Stoner, of the Bengal Artillery. My sister Julia and I were twins, and we were only two years old at the time of my mother's re-marriage. She had a considerable sum of money -- not less than 1000 pounds a year -- and this she bequeathed to Dr. Roylott entirely while we resided with him, with a provision that a certain annual sum should be allowed to each of us in the event of our marriage. Shortly after our return to England my mother died -- she was killed eight years ago in a railway accident near Crewe. Dr. Roylott then abandoned his attempts to establish himself in practice in London and took us to live with him in the old ancestral house at Stoke Moran. The money which my mother had left was enough for all our wants, and there seemed to be no obstacle to our happiness.

"But a terrible change came over our stepfather about this time. Instead of making friends and exchanging visits with our neighbors, who had at first been overjoyed to see a Roylott of Stoke Moran back in the old family seat, he shut himself up in his house and seldom came out save to indulge in ferocious quarrels with whoever might cross his path. Violence of temper approaching to mania has been hereditary in the men of the family, and in my stepfather's case it had, I believe, been intensified by his long residence in the tropics. A series of disgraceful brawls took place, two of which ended in the police-court, until at last he became the terror of the village, and the folks would fly at his approach, for he is a man of immense strength, and absolutely uncontrollable in his anger.

"Last week he hurled the local blacksmith over a parapet into a stream, and it was only by paying over all the money which I could gather together that I was able to avert another public exposure. He had no friends at all save the wandering gypsies, and he would give these vagabonds leave to encamp upon the few acres of bramble-covered land which represent the family estate, and would accept in return the hospitality of their tents, wandering away with them sometimes for weeks on end. He has a passion also for Indian animals, which are sent over to him by a correspondent, and he has at this moment a cheetah and a baboon, which wander freely over his grounds and are feared by the villagers almost as much as their master.

"You can imagine from what I say that my poor sister Julia and I had no great pleasure in our lives. No servant would stay with us, and for a long time we did all the work of the house. She was but thirty at the time of her death, and yet her hair had already begun to whiten, even as mine has."

"Your sister is dead, then?"

"She died just two years ago, and it is of her death that I wish to speak to you. You can understand that, living the life which I have described, we were little likely to see anyone of our own age and position. We had, however, an aunt, my mother's maiden sister, Miss Honoria Westphail, who lives near Harrow, and we were occasionally allowed to pay short visits at this lady's house. Julia went there at Christmas two years ago, and met there a half-pay major of marines, to whom she became engaged. My stepfather learned of the engagement when my sister returned and offered no objection to the marriage; but within a fortnight of the day which had been fixed for the wedding, the terrible event occurred which has deprived me of my only companion."

Sherlock Holmes had been leaning back in his chair with his eyes closed and his head sunk in a cushion, but he half opened his lids now and glanced across at his visitor.

"Pray be precise as to details," said he.

"It is easy for me to be so, for every event of that dreadful time is seared into my memory. The manor-house is, as I have already said, very old, and only one wing is now inhabited. The bedrooms in this wing are on the ground floor, the sitting-rooms being in the central block of the buildings. Of these bedrooms the first is Dr. Roylott's, the second my sister's, and the third my own. There is no communication between them, but they all open out into the same corridor. Do I make myself plain?"

"Perfectly so."

"The windows of the three rooms open out upon the lawn. That fatal night Dr. Roylott had gone to his room early, though we knew that he had not retired to rest, for my sister was troubled by the smell of the strong Indian cigars which it was his custom to smoke. She left her room, therefore, and came into mine, where she sat for some time, chatting about her approaching wedding. At eleven o'clock she rose to leave me, but she paused at the door and looked back.

"'Tell me, Helen,' said she, 'have you ever heard anyone whistle in the dead of the night?'

"'Never,' said I.

"'I suppose that you could not possibly whistle, yourself, in your sleep?'

"'Certainly not. But why?'

"'Because during the last few nights I have always, about three in the morning, heard a low, clear whistle. I am a light sleeper, and it has awakened me. I cannot tell where it came from perhaps from the next room, perhaps from the lawn. I thought that I would just ask you whether you had heard it.'

"'No, I have not. It must be those wretched gypsies in the plantation.'

"'Very likely. And yet if it were on the lawn, I wonder that you did not hear it also.'

"'Ah, but I sleep more heavily than you.'

"'Well, it is of no great consequence, at any rate.' She smiled back at me, closed my door, and a few moments later I heard her key turn in the lock."

"Indeed," said Holmes. "Was it your custom always to lock yourselves in at night?"

"Always."

"And why?"

"I think that I mentioned to you that the doctor kept a cheetah and a baboon. We had no feeling of security unless our doors were locked."

"Quite so. Pray proceed with your statement."

"I could not sleep that night. A vague feeling of impending misfortune impressed me. My sister and I, you will recollect, were twins, and you know how subtle are the links which bind two souls which are so closely allied. It was a wild night. The wind was howling outside, and the rain was beating and splashing against the windows. Suddenly, amid all the hubbub of the gale, there burst forth the wild scream of a terrified woman. I knew that it was my sister's voice. I sprang from my bed, wrapped a shawl round me, and rushed into the corridor. As I opened my door I seemed to hear a low whistle, such as my sister described, and a few moments later a clanging sound, as if a mass of metal had fallen. As I ran down the passage, my sister's door was unlocked, and revolved slowly upon its hinges. I stared at it horror-stricken, not knowing what was about to issue from it. By the light of the corridor-lamp I saw my sister appear at the opening, her face blanched with terror, her hands groping for help, her whole figure swaying to and fro like that of a drunkard. I ran to her and threw my arms round her, but at that moment her knees seemed to give way and she fell to the ground. She writhed as one who is in terrible pain, and her limbs were dreadfully convulsed. At first I thought that she had not recognized me, but as I bent over her she suddenly shrieked out in a voice which I shall never forget, 'Oh, my God! Helen! It was the band! The speckled band!' There was something else which she would fain have said, and she stabbed with her finger into the air in the direction of the doctor's room, but a fresh convulsion seized her and choked her words. I rushed out, calling loudly for my stepfather, and I met him hastening from his room in his dressing-gown. When he reached my sister's side she was unconscious, and though he poured brandy down her throat and sent for medical aid from the village, all efforts were in vain, for she slowly sank and died without having recovered her consciousness. Such was the dreadful end of my beloved sister."

"One moment," said Holmes, "are you sure about this whistle and metallic sound? Could you swear to it?"

"That was what the county coroner asked me at the inquiry. It is my strong impression that I heard it, and yet, among the crash of the gale and the creaking of an old house, I may possibly have been deceived."

"Was your sister dressed?"

"No, she was in her night-dress. In her right hand was found the charred stump of a match, and in her left a match-box."

"Showing that she had struck a light and looked about her when the alarm took place. That is important. And what conclusions did the coroner come to?"

"He investigated the case with great care, for Dr. Roylott's conduct had long been notorious in the county, but he was unable to find any satisfactory cause of death. My evidence showed that the door had been fastened upon the inner side, and the windows were blocked by old-fashioned shutters with broad iron bars, which were secured every night. The walls were carefully sounded, and were shown to be quite solid all round, and the flooring was also thoroughly examined, with the same result. The chimney is wide, but is barred up by four large staples. It is certain, therefore, that my sister was quite alone when she met her end. Besides, there were no marks of any violence upon her."

"How about poison?"

"The doctors examined her for it, but without success."

"What do you think that this unfortunate lady died of, then?"

"It is my belief that she died of pure fear and nervous shock, though what it was that frightened her I cannot imagine."

"Were there gypsies in the plantation at the time?"

"Yes, there are nearly always some there."

"Ah, and what did you gather from this allusion to a band -- a speckled band?"

"Sometimes I have thought that it was merely the wild talk of delirium, sometimes that it may have referred to some band of people, perhaps to these very gypsies in the plantation. I do not know whether the spotted handkerchiefs which so many of them wear over their heads might have suggested the strange adjective which she used."

Holmes shook his head like a man who is far from being satisfied.

"These are very deep waters," said he; "pray go on with your narrative."

"Two years have passed since then, and my life has been until lately lonelier than ever. A month ago, however, a dear friend, whom I have known for many years, has done me the honor to ask my hand in marriage. His name is Armitage -- Percy Armitage -- the second son of Mr. Armitage, of Crane Water, near Reading. My stepfather has offered no opposition to the match, and we are to be married in the course of the spring. Two days ago some repairs were started in the west wing of the building, and my bedroom wall has been pierced, so that I have had to move into the chamber in which my sister died, and to sleep in the very bed in which she slept. Imagine, then, my thrill of terror when last night, as I lay awake, thinking over her terrible fate, I suddenly heard in the silence of the night the low whistle which had been the herald of her own death. I sprang up and lit the lamp, but nothing was to be seen in the room. I was too shaken to go to bed again, however, so I dressed, and as soon as it was daylight I slipped down, got a dog-cart at the Crown Inn, which is opposite, and drove to Leatherhead, from whence I have come on this morning with the one object of seeing you and asking your advice."

"You have done wisely," said my friend. "But have you told me all?"

"Yes, all."

"Miss Roylott, you have not. You are screening your stepfather."

"Why, what do you mean?"

For answer Holmes pushed back the frill of black lace which fringed the hand that lay upon our visitor's knee. Five little livid spots, the marks of four fingers and a thumb, were printed upon the white wrist.

"You have been cruelly used," said Holmes.

The lady colored deeply and covered over her injured wrist. "He is a hard man," she said, "and perhaps he hardly knows his own strength."

There was a long silence, during which Holmes leaned his chin upon his hands and stared into the crackling fire.

"This is a very deep business," he said at last. "There are a thousand details which I should desire to know before I decide upon our course of action. Yet we have not a moment to lose. If we were to come to Stoke Moran to-day, would it be possible for us to see over these rooms without the knowledge of your stepfather?"

"As it happens, he spoke of coming into town to-day upon some most important business. It is probable that he will be away all day, and that there would be nothing to disturb you. We have a housekeeper now, but she is old and foolish, and I could easily get her out of the way."

"Excellent. You are not averse to this trip, Watson?"

"By no means."

"Then we shall both come. What are you going to do yourself?"

"I have one or two things which I would wish to do now that I am in town. But I shall return by the twelve o'clock train, so as to be there in time for your coming."

"And you may expect us early in the afternoon. I have myself some small business matters to attend to. Will you not wait and breakfast?"

"No, I must go. My heart is lightened already since I have confided my trouble to you. I shall look forward to seeing you again this afternoon." She dropped her thick black veil over her face and glided from the room.

"And what do you think of it all, Watson?" asked Sherlock Holmes, leaning back in his chair.

"It seems to me to be a most dark and sinister business."

"Dark enough and sinister enough."

"Yet if the lady is correct in saying that the flooring and walls are sound, and that the door, window, and chimney are impassable, then her sister must have been undoubtedly alone when she met her mysterious end."

"What becomes, then, of these nocturnal whistles, and what of the very peculiar words of the dying woman?"

"I cannot think."

"When you combine the ideas of whistles at night, the presence of a band of gypsies who are on intimate terms with this old doctor, the fact that we have every reason to believe that the doctor has an interest in preventing his stepdaughter's marriage, the dying allusion to a band, and, finally, the fact that Miss Helen Stoner heard a metallic clang, which might have been caused by one of those metal bars that secured the shutters falling back into its place, I think that there is good ground to think that the mystery may be cleared along those lines."

"But what, then, did the gypsies do?"

"I cannot imagine."

"I see many objections to any such theory."

"And so do I. It is precisely for that reason that we are going to Stoke Moran this day. I want to see whether the objections are fatal, or if they may be explained away. But what in the name of the devil!"

The ejaculation had been drawn from my companion by the fact that our door had been suddenly dashed open, and that a huge man had framed himself in the aperture. His costume was a peculiar mixture of the professional and of the agricultural, having a black top-hat, a long frock-coat, and a pair of high gaiters, with a hunting-crop swinging in his hand. So tall was he that his hat actually brushed the cross bar of the doorway, and his breadth seemed to span it across from side to side. A large face, seared with a thousand wrinkles, burned yellow with the sun, and marked with every evil passion, was turned from one to the other of us, while his deep-set, bile-shot eyes, and his high, thin, fleshless nose, gave him somewhat the resemblance to a fierce old bird of prey.

"Which of you is Holmes?" asked this apparition.

"My name, sir; but you have the advantage of me," said my companion quietly.

"I am Dr. Grimesby Roylott, of Stoke Moran."

"Indeed, Doctor," said Holmes blandly. "Pray take a seat."

"I will do nothing of the kind. My stepdaughter has been here. I have traced her. What has she been saying to you?"

"It is a little cold for the time of the year," said Holmes.

"What has she been saying to you?" screamed the old man furiously.

"But I have heard that the crocuses promise well," continued my companion imperturbably.

"Ha! You put me off, do you?" said our new visitor, taking a step forward and shaking his hunting-crop. "I know you, you scoundrel! I have heard of you before. You are Holmes, the meddler."

My friend smiled.

"Holmes, the busybody!"

His smile broadened.

"Holmes, the Scotland Yard Jack-in-office!"

Holmes chuckled heartily. "Your conversation is most entertaining," said he. "When you go out close the door, for there is a decided draught."

"I will go when I have said my say. Don't you dare to meddle with my affairs. I know that Miss Stoner has been here. I traced her! I am a dangerous man to fall foul of! See here." He stepped swiftly forward, seized the poker, and bent it into a curve with his huge brown hands.

"See that you keep yourself out of my grip," he snarled, and hurling the twisted poker into the fireplace he strode out of the room.

"He seems a very amiable person," said Holmes, laughing. "I am not quite so bulky, but if he had remained I might have shown him that my grip was not much more feeble than his own." As he spoke he picked up the steel poker and, with a sudden effort, straightened it out again.

"Fancy his having the insolence to confound me with the official detective force! This incident gives zest to our investigation, however, and I only trust that our little friend will not suffer from her imprudence in allowing this brute to trace her. And now, Watson, we shall order breakfast, and afterwards I shall walk down to Doctors' Commons, where I hope to get some data which may help us in this matter."

It was nearly one o'clock when Sherlock Holmes returned from his excursion. He held in his hand a sheet of blue paper, scrawled over with notes and figures.

"I have seen the will of the deceased wife," said he. "To determine its exact meaning I have been obliged to work out the present prices of the investments with which it is concerned. The total income, which at the time of the wife's death was little short of 1100 pounds, is now, through the fall in agricultural prices, not more than 750 pounds. Each daughter can claim an income of 250 pounds, in case of marriage. It is evident, therefore, that if both girls had married, this beauty would have had a mere pittance, while even one of them would cripple him to a very serious extent. My morning's work has not been wasted, since it has proved that he has the very strongest motives for standing in the way of anything of the sort. And now, Watson, this is too serious for dawdling, especially as the old man is aware that we are interesting ourselves in his affairs; so if you are ready, we shall call a cab and drive to Waterloo. I should be very much obliged if you would slip your revolver into your pocket. An Eley's No. 2 is an excellent argument with gentlemen who can twist steel pokers into knots. That and a tooth-brush are, I think, all that we need."

At Waterloo we were fortunate in catching a train for Leatherhead, where we hired a trap at the station inn and drove for four or five miles through the lovely Surrey laries. It was a perfect day, with a bright sun and a few fleecy clouds in the heavens. The trees and wayside hedges were just throwing out their first green shoots, and the air was full of the pleasant smell of the moist earth. To me at least there was a strange contrast between the sweet promise of the spring and this sinister quest upon which we were engaged. My companion sat in the front of the trap, his arms folded, his hat pulled down over his eyes, and his chin sunk upon his breast, buried in the deepest thought. Suddenly, however, he started, tapped me on the shoulder, and pointed over the meadows

"Look there!" said he.

A heavily timbered park stretched up in a gentle slope, thickening into a grove at the highest point. From amid the branches there jutted out the gray gables and high roof-tree of a very old mansion.

"Stoke Moran?" said he.

"Yes, sir, that be the house of Dr. Grimesby Roylott," remarked the driver.

"There is some building going on there," said Holmes; "that is where we are going."

"There's the village," said the driver, pointing to a cluster of roofs some distance to the left; "but if you want to get to the house, you'll find it shorter to get over this stile, and so by the foot-path over the fields. There it is, where the lady is walking."

"And the lady, I fancy, is Miss Stoner," observed Holmes, shading his eyes. "Yes, I think we had better do as you suggest."

We got off, paid our fare, and the trap rattled back on its way to Leatherhead.

"I thought it as well," said Holmes as we climbed the stile, "that this fellow should think we had come here as architects, or on some definite business. It may stop his gossip. Good-afternoon, Miss Stoner. You see that we have been as good as our word."

Our client of the morning had hurried forward to meet us with a face which spoke her joy. "I have been waiting so eagerly for you," she cried, shaking hands with us warmly. "All has turned out splendidly. Dr. Roylott has gone to town, and it is unlikely that he will be back before evening."

"We have had the pleasure of making the doctor's acquaintance," said Holmes, and in a few words he sketched out what had occurred. Miss Stoner turned white to the lips as she listened.

"Good heavens!" she cried, "he has followed me, then."

"So it appears."

"He is so cunning that I never know when I am safe from him. What will he say when he returns?"

"He must guard himself, for he may find that there is someone more cunning than himself upon his track. You must lock yourself up from him to-night. If he is violent, we shall take you away to your aunt's at Harrow. Now, we must make the best use of our time, so kindly take us at once to the rooms which we are to examine."

The building was of gray, lichen-blotched stone, with a high central portion and two curving wings, like the claws of a crab, thrown out on each side. In one of these wings the windows were broken and blocked with wooden boards, while the roof was partly caved in, a picture of ruin. The central portion was in little better repair, but the right-hand block was comparatively modern, and the blinds in the windows, with the blue smoke curling up from the chimneys, showed that this was where the family resided. Some scaffolding had been erected against the end wall, and the stone-work had been broken into, but there were no signs of any workmen at the moment of our visit. Holmes walked slowly up and down the ill-trimmed lawn and examined with deep attention the outsides of the windows.

"This, I take it, belongs to the room in which you used to sleep, the center one to your sister's, and the one next to the main building to Dr. Roylott's chamber?"

"Exactly so. But I am now sleeping in the middle one."

"Pending the alterations, as I understand. By the way, there does not seem to be any very pressing need for repairs at that end wall."

"There were none. I believe that it was an excuse to move me from my room."

"Ah! that is suggestive. Now, on the other side of this narrow wing runs the corridor from which these three rooms open. There are windows in it, of course?"

"Yes, but very small ones. Too narrow for anyone to pass through."

"As you both locked your doors at night, your rooms were unapproachable from that side. Now, would you have the kindness to go into your room and bar your shutters?"

Miss Stoner did so, and Holmes, after a careful examination through the open window, endeavored in every way to force the shutter open, but without success. There was no slit through which a knife could be passed to raise the bar. Then with his lens he tested the hinges, but they were of solid iron, built firmly into the massive masonry. "Hum!" said he, scratching his chin in some perplexity, "my theory certainly presents some difficulties. No one could pass these shutters if they were bolted. Well, we shall see if the inside throws any light upon the matter."

A small side door led into the whitewashed corridor from which the three bedrooms opened. Holmes refused to examine the third chamber, so we passed at once to the second, that in which Miss Stoner was now sleeping, and in which her sister had met with her fate. It was a homely little room, with a low ceiling and a gaping fireplace, after the fashion of old country-houses. A brown chest of drawers stood in one corner, a narrow white-counterpaned bed in another, and a dressing-table on the left-hand side of the window. These articles, with two small wicker-work chairs, made up all the furniture in the room save for a square of Wilton carpet in the center. The boards round and the paneling of the walls were of brown, worm-eaten oak, so old and discolored that it may have dated from the original building of the house. Holmes drew one of the chairs into a corner and sat silent, while his eyes travelled round and round and up and down, taking in every detail of the apartment.

"Where does that bell communicate with?" he asked at last pointing to a thick belt-rope which hung down beside the bed, the tassel actually lying upon the pillow.

"It goes to the housekeeper's room."

"It looks newer than the other things?"

"Yes, it was only put there a couple of years ago."

"Your sister asked for it, I suppose?"

"No, I never heard of her using it. We used always to get what we wanted for ourselves."

"Indeed, it seemed unnecessary to put so nice a bell-pull there. You will excuse me for a few minutes while I satisfy myself as to this floor." He threw himself down upon his face with his lens in his hand and crawled swiftly backward and forward, examining minutely the cracks between the boards. Then he did the same with the wood-work with which the chamber was paneled. Finally he walked over to the bed and spent some time in staring at it and in running his eye up and down the wall. Finally he took the bell-rope in his hand and gave it a brisk tug.

"Why, it's a dummy," said he.

"Won't it ring?"

"No, it is not even attached to a wire. This is very interesting. You can see now that it is fastened to a hook just above where the little opening for the ventilator is."

"How very absurd! I never noticed that before."

"Very strange!" muttered Holmes, pulling at the rope. "There are one or two very singular points about this room. For example, what a fool a builder must be to open a ventilator into another room, when, with the same trouble, he might have communicated with the outside air!"

"That is also quite modern," said the lady.

"Done about the same time as the bell-rope?" remarked Holmes.

"Yes, there were several little changes carried out about that time."

"They seem to have been of a most interesting character -- dummy bell-ropes, and ventilators which do not ventilate. With your permission, Miss Stoner, we shall now carry our researches into the inner apartment."

Dr. Grimesby Roylott's chamber was larger than that of his step-daughter, but was as plainly furnished. A camp-bed, a small wooden shelf full of books, mostly of a technical character an armchair beside the bed, a plain wooden chair against the wall, a round table, and a large iron safe were the principal things which met the eye. Holmes walked slowly round and examined each and all of them with the keenest interest.

"What's in here?" he asked, tapping the safe.

"My stepfather's business papers."

"Oh! you have seen inside, then?"

"Only once, some years ago. I remember that it was full of papers."

"There isn't a cat in it, for example?"

"No. What a strange idea!"

"Well, look at this!" He took up a small saucer of milk which stood on the top of it.

"No; we don't keep a cat. But there is a cheetah and a baboon."

"Ah, yes, of course! Well, a cheetah is just a big cat, and yet a saucer of milk does not go very far in satisfying its wants, I daresay. There is one point which I should wish to determine." He squatted down in front of the wooden chair and examined the seat of it with the greatest attention.

"Thank you. That is quite settled," said he, rising and putting his lens in his pocket. "Hello! Here is something interesting!"

The object which had caught his eye was a small dog lash hung on one corner of the bed. The lash, however, was curled upon itself and tied so as to make a loop of whipcord.

"What do you make of that, Watson?"

"It's a common enough lash. But I don't know why if should be tied."

"That is not quite so common, is it? Ah, me! it's a wicked world, and when a clever man turns his brains to crime it is the worst of all. I think that I have seen enough now, Miss Stoner, and with your permission we shall walk out upon the lawn."

I had never seen my friend's face so grim or his brow so dark as it was when we turned from the scene of this investigation. We had walked several times up and down the lawn, neither Miss Stoner nor myself liking to break in upon his thoughts before he roused himself from his reverie.

"It is very essential, Miss Stoner," said he, "that you should absolutely follow my advice in every respect."

"I shall most certainly do so."

"The matter is too serious for any hesitation. Your life may depend upon your compliance."

"I assure you that I am in your hands."

"In the first place, both my friend and I must spend the night in your room."

Both Miss Stoner and I gazed at him in astonishment.

"Yes, it must be so. Let me explain. I believe that that is the village inn over there?"

"Yes, that is the Crown."

"Very good. Your windows would be visible from there?"

"Certainly."

"You must confine yourself to your room, on pretense of a headache, when your stepfather comes back. Then when you hear him retire for the night, you must open the shutters of your window, undo the hasp, put your lamp there as a signal to us, and then withdraw quietly with everything which you are likely to want into the room which you used to occupy. I have no doubt that, in spite of the repairs, you could manage there for one night."

"Oh, yes, easily."

"The rest you will leave in our hands."

"But what will you do?"

"We shall spend the night in your room, and we shall investigate the cause of this noise which has disturbed you."

"I believe, Mr. Holmes, that you have already made up your mind," said Miss Stoner, laying her hand upon my companion's sleeve.

"Perhaps I have."

"Then, for pity's sake, tell me what was the cause of my sister's death."

"I should prefer to have clearer proofs before I speak."

"You can at least tell me whether my own thought is correct, and if she died from some sudden fright."

"No, I do not think so. I think that there was probably some more tangible cause. And now, Miss Stoner, we must leave you for if Dr. Roylott returned and saw us our journey would be in vain. Good-bye, and be brave, for if you will do what I have told you you may rest assured that we shall soon drive away the dangers that threaten you."

Sherlock Holmes and I had no difficulty in engaging a bedroom and sitting-room at the Crown Inn. They were on the upper floor, and from our window we could command a view of the avenue gate, and of the inhabited wing of Stoke Moran Manor House. At dusk we saw Dr. Grimesby Roylott drive past, his huge form looming up beside the little figure of the lad who drove him. The boy had some slight difficulty in undoing the heavy iron gates, and we heard the hoarse roar of the doctor's voice and saw the fury with which he shook his clinched fists at him. The trap drove on, and a few minutes later we saw a sudden light spring up among the trees as the lamp was lit in one of the sitting-rooms.

"Do you know, Watson," said Holmes as we sat together in the gathering darkness, "I have really some scruples as to taking you to-night. There is a distinct element of danger."

"Can I be of assistance?"

"Your presence might be invaluable."

"Then I shall certainly come."

"It is very kind of you."

"You speak of danger. You have evidently seen more in these rooms than was visible to me."

"No, but I fancy that I may have deduced a little more. I imagine that you saw all that I did."

"I saw nothing remarkable save the bell-rope, and what purpose that could answer I confess is more than I can imagine."

"You saw the ventilator, too?"

"Yes, but I do not think that it is such a very unusual thing to have a small opening between two rooms. It was so small that a rat could hardly pass through."

"I knew that we should find a ventilator before ever we came to Stoke Moran."

"My dear Holmes!"

"Oh, yes, I did. You remember in her statement she said that her sister could smell Dr. Roylott's cigar. Now, of course that suggested at once that there must be a communication between the two rooms. It could only be a small one, or it would have been remarked upon at the coroner's inquiry. I deduced a ventilator."

"But what harm can there be in that?"

"Well, there is at least a curious coincidence of dates. A ventilator is made, a cord is hung, and a lady who sleeps in the bed dies. Does not that strike you?"

"I cannot as yet see any connection."

"Did you observe anything very peculiar about that bed?"

"No."

"It was clamped to the floor. Did you ever see a bed fastened like that before?"

"I cannot say that I have."

"The lady could not move her bed. It must always be in the same relative position to the ventilator and to the rope -- or so we may call it, since it was clearly never meant for a bell-pull."

"Holmes," I cried, "I seem to see dimly what you are hinting at. We are only just in time to prevent some subtle and horrible crime."

"Subtle enough and horrible enough. When a doctor does go wrong he is the first of criminals. He has nerve and he has knowledge. Palmer and Pritchard were among the heads of their profession. This man strikes even deeper, but I think, Watson, that we shall be able to strike deeper still. But we shall have horrors enough before the night is over; for goodness' sake let us have a quiet pipe and turn our minds for a few hours to something more cheerful."

About nine o'clock the light among the trees was extinguished, and all was dark in the direction of the Manor House. Two hours passed slowly away, and then, suddenly, just at the stroke of eleven, a single bright light shone out right in front of us.

"That is our signal," said Holmes, springing to his feet; "it comes from the middle window."

As we passed out he exchanged a few words with the landlord, explaining that we were going on a late visit to an acquaintance, and that it was possible that we might spend the night there. A moment later we were out on the dark road, a chill wind blowing in our faces, and one yellow light twinkling in front of us through the gloom to guide us on our somber errand.

There was little difficulty in entering the grounds, for unrepaired breaches gaped in the old park wall. Making our way among the trees, we reached the lawn, crossed it, and were about to enter through the window when out from a clump of laurel bushes there darted what seemed to be a hideous and distorted child, who threw itself upon the grass with writhing limbs and then ran swiftly across the lawn into the darkness.

"My God!" I whispered; "did you see it?"

Holmes was for the moment as startled as I. His hand closed like a vise upon my wrist in his agitation. Then he broke into a low laugh and put his lips to my ear.

"It is a nice household," he murmured. "That is the baboon."

I had forgotten the strange pets which the doctor affected. There was a cheetah, too; perhaps we might find it upon our shoulders at any moment. I confess that I felt easier in my mind when, after following Holmes's example and slipping off my shoes, I found myself inside the bedroom. My companion noiselessly closed the shutters, moved the lamp onto the table, and cast his eyes round the room. All was as we had seen it in the daytime. Then creeping up to me and making a trumpet of his hand, he whispered into my ear again so gently that it was all that I could do to distinguish the words:

"The least sound would be fatal to our plans."

I nodded to show that I had heard.

"We must sit without light. He would see it through the ventilator."

I nodded again.

"Do not go asleep; your very life may depend upon it. Have your pistol ready in case we should need it. I will sit on the side of the bed, and you in that chair."

I took out my revolver and laid it on the corner of the table.

Holmes had brought up a long thin cane, and this he placed upon the bed beside him. By it he laid the box of matches and the stump of a candle. Then he turned down the lamp, and we were left in darkness.

How shall I ever forget that dreadful vigil? I could not hear a sound, not even the drawing of a breath, and yet I knew that my companion sat open-eyed, within a few feet of me, in the same state of nervous tension in which I was myself. The shutters cut off the least ray of light, and we waited in absolute darkness.

From outside came the occasional cry of a night-bird, and once at our very window a long drawn catlike whine, which told us that the cheetah was indeed at liberty. Far away we could hear the deep tones of the parish clock, which boomed out every quarter of an hour. How long they seemed, those quarters! Twelve struck, and one and two and three, and still we sat waiting silently for whatever might befall.

Suddenly there was the momentary gleam of a light up in the direction of the ventilator, which vanished immediately, but was succeeded by a strong smell of burning oil and heated metal. Someone in the next room had lit a dark-lantern. I heard a gentle sound of movement, and then all was silent once more, though the smell grew stronger. For half an hour I sat with straining ears. Then suddenly another sound became audible -- a very gentle, soothing sound, like that of a small jet of steam escaping continually from a kettle. The instant that we heard it, Holmes sprang from the bed, struck a match, and lashed furiously with his cane at the bell-pull.

"You see it, Watson?" he yelled. "You see it?"

But I saw nothing. At the moment when Holmes struck the light I heard a low, clear whistle, but the sudden glare flashing into my weary eyes made it impossible for me to tell what it was at which my friend lashed so savagely. I could, however, see that his face was deadly pale and filled with horror and loathing. He had ceased to strike and was gazing up at the ventilator when suddenly there broke from the silence of the night the most horrible cry to which I have ever listened. It swelled up louder and louder, a hoarse yell of pain and fear and anger all mingled in the one dreadful shriek. They say that away down in the village, and even in the distant parsonage, that cry raised the sleepers from their beds. It struck cold to our hearts, and I stood gazing at Holmes, and he at me, until the last echoes of it had died away into the silence from which it rose.

"What can it mean?" I gasped.

"It means that it is all over," Holmes answered. "And perhaps, after all, it is for the best. Take your pistol, and we will enter Dr. Roylott's room."

With a grave face he lit the lamp and led the way down the corridor. Twice he struck at the chamber door without any reply from within. Then he turned the handle and entered, I at his heels, with the cocked pistol in my hand.

It was a singular sight which met our eyes. On the table stood a dark-lantern with the shutter half open, throwing a brilliant beam of light upon the iron safe, the door of which was ajar. Beside this table, on the wooden chair, sat Dr. Grimesby Roylott clad in a long gray dressing-gown, his bare ankles protruding beneath, and his feet thrust into red heelless Turkish slippers. Across his lap lay the short stock with the long lash which we had noticed during the day. His chin was cocked upward and his eyes were fixed in a dreadful, rigid stare at the corner of the ceiling. Round his brow he had a peculiar yellow band, with brownish speckles, which seemed to be bound tightly round his head. As we entered he made neither sound nor motion.

"The band! the speckled band!" whispered Holmes.

I took a step forward. In an instant his strange headgear began to move, and there reared itself from among his hair the squat diamond-shaped head and puffed neck of a loathsome serpent.

"It is a swamp adder!" cried Holmes; "the deadliest snake in India. He has died within ten seconds of being bitten. Violence does, in truth, recoil upon the violent, and the schemer falls into the pit which he digs for another. Let us thrust this creature back into its den, and we can then remove Miss Stoner to some place of shelter and let the county police know what has happened."

As he spoke he drew the dog-whip swiftly from the dead man's lap, and throwing the noose round the reptile's neck he drew it from its horrid perch and, carrying it at arm's length, threw it into the iron safe, which he closed upon it.

Such are the true facts of the death of Dr. Grimesby Roylott, of Stoke Moran. It is not necessary that I should prolong a narrative which has already run to too great a length by telling how we broke the sad news to the terrified girl, how we conveyed her by the morning train to the care of her good aunt at Harrow, of how the slow process of official inquiry came to the conclusion that the doctor met his fate while indiscreetly playing with a dangerous pet. The little which I had yet to learn of the case was told me by Sherlock Holmes as we travelled back next day.

"I had," said he, "come to an entirely erroneous conclusion which shows, my dear Watson, how dangerous it always is to reason from insufficient data. The presence of the gypsies, and the use of the word 'band,' which was used by the poor girl, no doubt to explain the appearance which she had caught a hurried glimpse of by the light of her match, were sufficient to put me upon an entirely wrong scent. I can only claim the merit that I instantly reconsidered my position when, however, it became clear to me that whatever danger threatened an occupant of the room could not come either from the window or the door. My attention was speedily drawn, as I have already remarked to you, to this ventilator, and to the bell-rope which hung down to the bed. The discovery that this was a dummy, and that the bed was clamped to the floor, instantly gave rise to the suspicion that the rope was there as a bridge for something passing through the hole and coming to the bed. The idea of a snake instantly occurred to me, and when I coupled it with my knowledge that the doctor was furnished with a supply of creatures from India, I felt that I was probably on the right track. The idea of using a form of poison which could not possibly be discovered by any chemical test was just such a one as would occur to a clever and ruthless man who had had an Eastern training. The rapidity with which such a poison would take effect would also, from his point of view, be an advantage. It would be a sharp-eyed coroner, indeed, who could distinguish the two little dark punctures which would show where the poison fangs had done their work. Then I thought of the whistle. Of course he must recall the snake before the morning light revealed it to the victim. He had trained it, probably by the use of the milk which we saw, to return to him when summoned. He would put it through this ventilator at the hour that he thought best, with the certainty that it would crawl down the rope and land on the bed. It might or might not bite the occupant, perhaps she might escape every night for a week, but sooner or later she must fall a victim.

"I had come to these conclusions before ever I had entered his room. An inspection of his chair showed me that he had been in the habit of standing on it, which of course would be necessary in order that he should reach the ventilator. The sight of the safe, the saucer of milk, and the loop of whipcord were enough to finally dispel any doubts which may have remained. The metallic clang heard by Miss Stoner was obviously caused by her stepfather hastily closing the door of his safe upon its terrible occupant. Having once made up my mind, you know the steps which I took in order to put the matter to the proof. I heard the creature hiss as I have no doubt that you did also, and I instantly lit the light and attacked it."

"With the result of driving it through the ventilator."

"And also with the result of causing it to turn upon its master at the other side. Some of the blows of my cane came home and roused its snakish temper, so that it flew upon the first person it saw. In this way I am no doubt indirectly responsible for Dr. Grimesby Roylott's death, and I cannot say that it is likely to weigh very heavily upon my conscience."

Hey readers: The first day of every month is *New Sherlock Day*. All New Sherlock Holmes Mysteries ebooks on Kindle will go on sale for 99 cents for one day only. Watch for it at the start of each month.

Made in the USA
San Bernardino, CA
31 October 2016